TROLLEY
No. 1852

EDWARD LEE

deadite
press

DEADITE PRESS
205 NE BRYANT
PORTLAND, OR 97211

AN ERASERHEAD PRESS COMPANY
WWW.ERASERHEADPRESS.COM

ISBN: 1-936383-17-9

"Trolley No. 1852" first appeared as a limited edition hardback by
Bloodletting Press, 2009.

Printed in the USA.

PROVIDENCE, RHODE ISLAND
1934

It was the spectral hump of Federal Hill that held the solitary man's gaze in capture, as oft it did, whene're he took to his work-desk in hopes of a Muse's whisper. The westward panes framed this inexpressible sight which rose two miles distant, and for reasons the lean, stoop-shouldered man could not explicate, beguiled his aesthetic senses as if to whelm them most utterly. Near dead-center of the roof-crowned rise stood the blackly bedrabbed hulk of St. John's Church, whose cold Gothic revival windows seemed to stare back at his gaze in a knowing despair. The man felt certain that one day this morbid and singularly sinister edifice would ignite the fuse of a new tale, yet as so often happens to the creatively inclined, there could be no tale without an accommodating catalyst.

The same could be said of his present scribbling, cursorily entitled "The Thing in the Moonlight," not a tale of itself but some rather desultory notes for one. It gravitated around a salient and very haunting image that had stricken him in a dream not far agone: a decrepit trolley-car rusting on its iron rails, slack power wires hanging overhead like dead umbilici. Ill-hued yellow paint mouldered around the vestibuled car, a colour akin to jaundice. A black and rather faded stencil identified the vehicle: *No. 1852.*

This dream-image disconcerted the man to no end, that and the image of the car's motorman who turned in shifting moonlight to display a heinous face that was nothing but a white fleshy cone tapering snout-like to a single blood-red tentacle . . .

Like the Gothic pile of the church, the blear-eyed man yearned to harness this image and then rein it into a tale of weird substantiality. But, lo, he knew without the proper catalyst, it would never be more than a page of fallow cacography. Such was the curse of a poor and aging scribe.

However, the door-slat's clatter alerted him to the arrival of the day's post, and instead of a nettlesome bill or—his worst fear—an eviction, he found a manila envelope awaiting. The upper-left corner bore no name but just a New York City address. From inside, his long thin fingers extracted a handsomely designed if not suspiciously suggestive magazine. Eloquent letters spelled its uncanny epithet EROTESQUE and a sub-heading: *Tales for the Selectively Bizarre.* A woodcut, quite byzantine in its elaborateness, comprised the cover in a style that seemed reminiscent of Frank Utpatel.

The *style,* he observed, yet hardly the content.

The woodcut shewed what—after a studied glance—could only be the silhouette of a winnowy, well-busted woman, undeniably nude and pruriently posed.

A neatly typed cover-letter read as thus:

Dear Mr. Lovecraft:

Forgive the intrusion of this unsolicited invitation. EROTESQUE is a privately-circulated periodical offering fictional fare of the most outre, iconoclastic, and unrepresentative, with eroticism as the central motif. Our readership demands sexually inspired fiction by the very best and most innovative authors of the day—authors such as yourself. Tales incorporating supernaturalism, experimental, da-da, alternate-history, and anti-authoritarian are most encouraged. Should you accept our offer, you will need to furnish a double-spaced typescript of no less than seven thousand words.

You need not worry about the potential controversy of your work appearing in a publication such as EROTESQUE (nor any attendant censorship ramifications); your contribution will be published pseudonymously, and we keep all pseudonyms under the most severe confidentiality. You may be surprised by how many of your peers publish with us on a regular basis.

We pay well above the industry standard; likewise we understand that authors of your admired caliber need not "audition" for inclusion, which is why we make the first-half payment in ADVANCE. Please find the enclosed cheque for $500.00. A second cheque for an identical sum will be rendered upon delivery of the ms. There is no deadline.

Should you not be interested, or are too pressed by your busy publishing schedule, simply return the cheque in the also-enclosed self-addressed, stamped envelope, and accept our thanks for your consideration.

We here at EROTESQUE would be honoured to have your preeminent work in our pages.

Cordially,
F. Wilcox

It would be superfluous to convey the extent of the writer's surprise and exuberance. With a $500 draft in hand, and another promised upon delivery? These sums singularly exceeded any in this poor scribe's professional history! *With all that filthy lucre?* he pondered, *I could pay the rest of my aunt's hospital bill AND cover our rent for a year!* When the offer's full weight sunk in, he actually shouted out a hackneyed and very ebullient, "Oh my God!"

He visibly trembled, then, when he sat down to read . . .

The magazine, as was manifest, existed for subversive readers, indeed. The man found the tales therein professionally rendered, adroitly and engagingly plotted, and flamboyantly conceived; however, it could not be denied. They were pornographic. Hence, the periodical's "private" circulation, for fiction such as this would be deemed illegal most anywhere. Desperate as he was for finances (this past winter he'd never been closer to the bread-line) he had to make the self-admission that he hardly approved of pornography; yet on the other hand . . . *Who am I to make judgments?* A violation of the law? More than likely. But he had to admit also that most of the contents of *Erotesque* displayed works of notable craft and fascinating imagery (however lewd that imagery may have been), and he had to admit likewise that the reading's wake left him aroused in a most primal and unmentionable manner—hence, the effect of the skills of the contributors. How quickly he decided to accept the offer he could not consciously say. Would he be prostituting his wee talents for money? Quite emphatically, he told himself, *No.* He saw this offer as a challenge, and no writer worth his salt ever turned down a challenge . . .

This was all ballyhoo, of course, a cheap rationalization. The writer had no verve to write pornography but he *needed the money,* damn it, and he was so tired of eating cold beans and week-old cheese!

So . . .

He thought the following soliloquy: *In my life of staggering travail, I've suffered humiliations and failures untold. Hectored as a child, forced to wear girls' smocks until the age of eight, socially stifled such that I was unable to graduate high school . . . For pittances, I've ghost-written for dolts and stoked their vain egos by allowing them to put their names on my prose and poetry. I bungled my way to termination as a door-to-door salesman, and I stuffed envelopes for mere pennies. I've stood like a lackwit drone in an unheated cubby selling movie tickets to snide, chuckling human vermin. Now, at the least, I would be something much of note:*

A pornographer!

But before he would scruple to live up to this F. Wilcox's adulatory opinion of his talents, he hunted through his fairly recent New York City telephone directory (which he keep on hand due to his frequent journeys there); naturally, there was no listing for *Erotesque* in the business segment; however . . .

Amongst the long string of Wilcoxes, he was encouraged to find a listing for a Wilcox, Frederick, at the same address as on the envelope. It made some sense that a publication of ribald literature would not have an official office, opting instead for the editor's home residence. He stroked his over-protuberant chin, thinking, *I suppose I could call Mr. Wilcox from the telephone at the boarding house across the way . . .*, but a second's contemplation deemed the action unnecessary. Instead came the resolve, *My writing is cut out for me. . .*, and what an energizing resolve it was!

Ah, but then exactly *what* would he write?

He'd already selected his *nom de plume;* it would be Winfield (his father's first name) Greene (his former wife's maiden name, which seemed splendidly appropriate for the author of pornography. The woman had been insatiable! She would impale herself on his groin in his sleep as though he were some nocturnal vending machine for her pleasure!) His tale's plot, though, was something else. Forcing conscious thought upon a creative target, he'd long learned, always resulted in an abject uselessness that drained the artist's confidence. He took to the streets, then, to stroll as he frequently did and hope that Mr. Freud's *sub*conscious might offer assistance. Some assistance, too, from Dante's Ladies of the Heavenly Spring might then soon follow, or so he aspired. No sooner had he turned down Benefit than some inklings began to kindle. There could be no utility whatever of his "Great Old Ones"—to do so would rupture the tale's pseudonymity!—but he could most appropriately re-apparel what his friend Little Belknap once called his "Cthulhuean Arena" with new garments of occultism. This ploy would not only camouflage the author's identity—and, hence, leave his personal repute uninjured—but also allow him to flex unused aesthetic muscles. As he usually did, he would create a protagonist who mirrored aspects of himself but then plunge him headlong into a most *un*usual concupiscent peril.

He chuckled—an annoying, high-pitched chuckle.

What fun the endeavor suddenly seemed!

Ah, but his success would demand more than an energized endeavor. *Blast! I need an idea!*

The generous bank cheque would take over a week to be honoured, but he did have a dollar or so on his person, and given that this was, of sorts, a celebration, he would so celebrate by rewarding his good fortune with a can of Heinz beans—quite satisfiably cold, he could tell you—and a can of Postum pre-ground coffee. (The other brands tasted like a cacodaemon's bile! *Ugh!*) So into the little Weybosset's shop he ventured, and made his purchases with pennies to spare from the shrewd-faced proprietor (quite a disestablishmentarian) who was blaming the government for the sudden rise of gasoline to seven cents per gallon and gold to nineteen dollars per ounce.

He smiled in silence with a nod and took his parcels just as a dour but well-attired man on the corpulent side stepped up and passed the rankled proprietor what looked like a pharmaceutical prescription, for there was a small apothecarium.

The proprietor scowled, disappeared into the back, then returned momentarily with what was undeniably a package of barrier prophylactics. He could even read the name-brand: GOODYEAR & HANCOCK - VULCANIZED CONTRACEPTIVE SHEATHS. The buyer seemed embarrassed to make this purchase and appeared doubly unnerved by the writer's presence as witness.

Though there was endless government talk of repealing the fifty-year-old Comstock Act (which banned the sale of these nefarious devices), he was heedlessly opposed to such a repeal. Violations were deemed a federal offense and carried a punishment—quite rightly, in his estimation—of five years imprisonment and hard labor. After losing so many young men in the Great War, and then a half-million more souls—oddly, mostly men—in the ghoulish Spanish Flu Epidemic, what was more ghastly than *encouraging* lustful hedonists to perpetrate their carnal traffic without any responsibility whatever? Certainly, America's strength came through the hard-work and innovation of its *people,* and circumventing necessary new births in the interest of bed-play seemed a howling affront to not only logic but a central morality. By law, these things, sometimes called "condoms" or, in the vernacular "skins," were only to be used by couples properly wedded for either the prevention of a pre-existing disease or to allow normal sexual congress between the husband and a wife likely to suffer medical complications in the event of pregnancy.

The embarrassed customer, after paying for his package, hurried his bulk toward the exit, but not before the vociferous proprietor called out, "Don't you be using those on any of them harlots out there, man! It's against the law! And them dirty women are full up with poxes that dissolve those things!"

The buyer couldn't have left in any more haste.

Next, the proprietor turned his scowl to the stooped writer. "You agree with me, don't'cha, mister?"

"Indubitably," he replied and left.

This, he was saddened to prehend, is what the "cracker barrels" of the good old days had become—unpleasant and often hostile rants. Confrontations were not his forte. But the proprietor could not be accused of exaggeration on one count: the gradually rising number of "harlots" plying their trade on these once-fine avenues. Back on the street, as the sinking sun commenced to flame across the roof-pocked horizon, he beheld the rancorous man's meaning. Visible at several corners loitered women of the illest repute, drab-faced and gaudily dressed waifs with hungry eyes. These pestilent and immoral urchins had grown in number to a dejecting degree, it seemed. Victims of President Hoover's economic failures or simply female loafers looking for easy earnings, he struggled not to judge. One thin bonneted creature with a vulpine grin beckoned him with her finger to cross the road. He did not oblige, of course; then another, brazenly brassiereless and sashaying in the uncomplimentary look of a Flapper, slowed her gait as she passed, and asked if he had a dollar for some of her company.

He assured her he did not.

Where are the constables when you need them!

As he stood in wait at the corner for several motors to putter by, he heard a trolley's bell clanging several blocks over, and then . . .

Then . . .

The moment strangely seized him. He stood immobile; a fugue seemed to drone in his head, much akin to the mad flute-pipings of his messenger-demigod Nyarlathotep; and all his powers of conjecture and mental function stalled in what could only be called utter aposiopesis . . .

Barrier prophylactics, the words thudded in his head, and then—

The toll of a distant trolley bell. Then—

Prostitutes . . .

These three images (two visual, one aural) shivered in his mind and gave root to an unmediated joyousness that caused him to actually shiver in place.

Why? you may ask.

They provided the creative lightning bolt so yearned for and so rare in a writer's life. These individual images lay in his hands the *catalyst* he'd been so desperately struggling for.

And it was in that irreducible division of a second that Howard Lovecraft had his story for Mr. Frederick Wilcox and the clandestine periodical known as *Erotesque.*

Within minutes he was back in his chamber, coffee on and pen in hand, writing his new tale . . .

TROLLEY NO. 1852

BY

WINFIELD GREENE

One

My name is Morgan Phillips, and I am recounting this experience in hopes that by doing so I might unburden my mind—and whatever beneficent memories I have left—of some of the venomous and imponderable images which stalk me ever still . . .

. . . for however long the earth shall last.

My relocation to New York (that denizen-abyss of stridence and foul smells) had been by necessity and not—I re-emphasize, *not*—due to the divestment of my position at Brown, as a professor of mythology and ancient histories, two years ago. The latter had been the work of this bungling and greed-induced calamity they are now calling the "Great Depression," whose attendant turmoil left no room for teachers of subjectivities. Only academicians skilled in mathematics, industry, and the sciences could be retained in such troubled times of bread lines and twenty-five-percent jobless rates. For the rest of us (history, literature, the arts) the coffers of higher learning were closed.

Instead, I ventured hither, to this mephitic necropolis of concrete, dirt, and clamour, in the steadfast hope of ascertaining the whereabouts of my sister and only sibling, Selina, who'd relocated here some five years ago for a $14-per-week accounting position with the well-known Monroe Clothiers chain. She would be twenty (eight now—seven years my junior) and with her youth had come the zeal of wanderlust. "I want *new* horizons, Morgan," she'd implored

13

five years afore with her over-bright eyes and buoyant enthusiasm. "*New* places to see and *new* people to meet, and *don't worry,* I'll write you every week!" So she had, for three years, until her unforeboding and quite energetic missives in the post had dropped off all at once in an eerie silence. Either Fate or the god Selina believed in but I did not had seen fit to parallel my sister's disappearance, nearly to the day, with my own woeful dismissal from Brown. I took the ten-six, with no hesitancy whatever, to Penn Station, and have been here ever since.

Or at least, in a *sense* . . .

It was in stifled shock that I first beheld this labyrinthine canyon of crime and leering, stubbled faces; shock that palsied my gait and numbed my mind—a seething urban *mass* of filthily attired bodies of clearly all ancestries save for the Anglican; bodies that moved shiftily through garbage-heaped streets pressed on either side by grimy concrete towers so spiring as to obfuscate the light of day—indeed a noisome Babel of movement, ill-will, and malodour; of sweat-shined foreheads and menacing scowls. Squalid ghettoblocks stretched shabbily betwixt skyscrapers too dizzying to look upward at; and the smell—the unsurceasing and absolutely maleficent *smell*— which imbued itself in my clothes and, I often suspected, my very pores. This—*city*—was not for my sensitive kind, but circumstances offered me little choice. I scrupled at once to take my place in the human *crush* so erroneously named for James II, the Duke of York, lest I be swallowed whole by its incogitable machinations.

That *Selina* had been so swallowed remained my most teeming fear.

Degradation after degradation pursued me posthaste—things I cannot, must not recount. Here squalor and hatred reigned supreme, for if the flumelike streets proved this evil urban pustule's veins, then surely the ignoble masses served as its blood. I will not say how my first pitiable meals came to my mouth; nor how oft misfortune nearly left me bloodied and broken-boned by mongrel hoodlums in nighted alleyways.

But my bounden duty to find Selina steeled my perseverance. Amid the stinking crowds of pick-pockets and fugitives, and amongst cramped, sunless thoroughfares sided by drear-paned walls zigzagged by clattery iron fire-escapes, I travailed first to secure 30-cent-per-hour employment at a reformed scrivenry; and an unutterably pestiferous "room" on 28th Street, for a half-dollar a day.

Time acclimated me to most of my inner horrors and my loath for what I could only metaphor as the societal elephantiasis in which I lived. Selina's rescue, in the very least as my strained mind envisioned it, was all that gave me the will to forge on. I fared well at my new post (a man of erudition? A university professor?) and rose up the few ladders of advancement that were extant; whereas I soon was promoted to night-office manager whose undesirable hours rewarded me with a modest pay increment. The enterprise, namely Bartleby & Sons, L.T.D., occupied the top floor of a rather Dickensian building that harkened from the middle of the Nineteenth Century, in the lower "meat-packers" borough. Of course, they'd long-since refitted materially with modern typing-machines, (chiefly Remington Model One's on which I'd grown adroit at Brown) and more recently curious devices of almost supernatural capability, called Mimeographs. My status quickly charged me with the overwatch of the night-staff: all stalwart men and women possessed of acceptable typing skills and an accurate eye, who'd been discarded from better posts by the all-pervading economic gloom. It was for the most part elder holographed documents of financial and governmental importance that we were charged with transcribing, from seven o'clock in evening to three-thirty or so in the morn.

As for Selina, however . . .

It necessitated less than a week's time to discern that the illustrious Monroe Clothiers chain was illustrious no more; the abrupt sign on the front doors announced that the enterprise had gone on "Holiday" much the same way as most banking institutions; in a more accurate manner of speaking: bankrupt, and all employees let go. Worse than that, by far, however, was my horror in learning that Selina's apartment building in the West Side had burned to the ground; though I was relieved to be informed by the New York Office of Public Safety that no deaths or injuries had been reported. Next, my forlorn sojourn through the mephitis piloted me to the local police precinct's Missing Persons Bureau. Here, to my abject despair, I was informed that said bureau was no longer operational due to budget decreases and the simple unserviceability of such a function. "You got any idea how many people 'disappear' with the economy the way it is?" my complaint was chastised by a surly sergeant at the desk. "Well do ya, bub?" Ultimately, of course, I could comprehend his point; in such dismal economic times, people moved on to unknown pastures they hoped would be greener but oft were not. *But Selina would've written me had she elected to relocate,* I knew full well. The granite-faced sergeant was unkind enough to add an acerbic statistical datum: "Lots'a women have took to sellin' thereselfs, ya know. What else they got when there's no jobs and bread's up to a dime'a half-loaf?" Then, another datum: "Oh, and bub? You do know that the murder and suicide rate's doubled since the Crash in '29, don't ya?"

When not tending my duties at the scrivenry, then, I walked . . .

Walked, I say, through every chasm, byway, and alley in vicinity to Selina's former home and place of employment; walked through the harrowing and ill-scented masses—that loathly, dead-faced human sprawl—thrusting forward my only photograph of Selina to random passersby and shop-keepers, coppers and vagrants alike, refugees and natural-born citizens—indeed, *anyone,* with the plea hot in my voice, "Have you seen this woman?"

None had.

When I'd covered the most logical geographical propinquities, an absence of alternatives forced me to proceed in depressingly widening radii. First what remained of Manhattan, then Queens, the Bronx, then ghastly Flatbush and the horrendous Brooklyn and its appalling appendage Red Hook full of leaning tenements and unrestrained hooliganism; Staten Island and its waves of cretins, then across the blackly gushing Hudson to Hoboken, Union City, and beyond. All, all to no avail. In no time, however, I became deft in all modes of travel (ferries, trolleys, motor-carriages) and during my scouring of the stolid, grey Brooklyn borough, even traveled in the impossible underground trains that had commenced in 1904, in particular this BRT Line; and then the reeking, flesh-packed 9th Avenue Line—these being deafening, subterrene contraptions they now called the Subway.

It was all I lived for, for I had nothing else: my indefatigable certainty that somewhere, out thither in this once fecund and beauteous Ilse of Manna-hata that the White Man had paved over with modern horrors called Progress, below the once-resplendent pristine-blue sky now soiled by hostile chatter and coal-smoke; *somewhere* amid all of this, Selina still lived and breathed.

Somewhere.

And though we're taught in our youth of the virtue of tenaciousness and faith (indeed, the very *Godliness* of it) I found instead of solace a soul-poisoning and ever-cresting cynicism that more and more graduated to outright nihilism. I became convinced that Nietzsche's chief tenet seethed in undeniablity; that there was no objective basis for truth. Here I was, standing in the middle of that pestilent, dirty-handed verity; the summation of all that mankind has risen to in multiple-millennia of evolvement; yes, yes, *this:* human feces in the open street; the vomit of vagabonds filling gutters like abscessed putrid evil rainwater; women so bereft of morality (and men too) that they'd sell their sex for a half-dollar, a dime, even a nickel; blood turning brown on unending concrete walls; thugs beating the maimed and the elderly for pittances in raging daylight; police turning quickly away from those most in need; one alley after the next, urine-imbued and clogged like demon-dens with cadaverously thin addicts puffing blank-eyed on opium or even injecting narcotics into their bodies through their veins; rats, rats, *droves* of them; and the lines and the lines and the lines of the dirty and the wretched and the sin-stained. Indeed, the pinnacle of mankind's knowledge and endeavor for ten-thousand years; this ghastly, irrevocable *horror.*

Too often I mused that if the stone-faced sergeant were abstractly correct, and that my faultless sister had reached the psychic saturation-point and succumbed to self-annihilation, I too might well soon follow.

Days of useless searches bled into smoke-sullied gloaming, for another night of monotonous labor which after interminable hours would then bleed back into days of more useless searches. I'd ride grim trolleys and wretch-piloted coaches, scouring every passing flinty face and scowling countenance in the dead hope that one would be Selina; walked soles off my very shoes searching still more, only to be rewarded by slipping on a bum's blood-marbled sputum or being bumped, shoved, and cursed at in a dozen hateful dialects by scores of hateful faces. Even the churches closed their doors to the uncontainable throng . . . God, indeed. What true *god* could turn his back on a woman as goodly as my sister and allow her to be sucked up, swallowed, and digested into this irredeemable abyss of stench, cacophony, and illicitness? How could any "Supreme Being" exist so coldly and unconscionably as to relinquish kind and life-praising souls as Selina to this metropolic spittoon of human wretchedness? Where eyes in my beloved and stately Providence shined in hope and kindredship, hither they only glimmered dully in turpitude and greed.

After two long years, then, my spirit was all but done. Evening time closed over me like a casket's lid, where then I labored in my cubby till my fingers raged in pain, only to know that the coming dawn would bring no surcease. Day after day, the clocks ticked in a semblance to dripping blood, and I felt as though my soul had metamorphosed to the blackest sand, spilling ever away through some morbid existential hour-glass that had no bottom.

When I slept I dreamt of the hangman's noose.

At my place of employ, I took care to befriend no one but instead oversaw the nightly duties of all with a stolid, vigilant face; anything less would be fraternization and, hence, unprofessional. On the same hand, my deflated spirit left me in no desire for comradeship. There was one soul, though, with whom I did feel something of a connexion: the sullen building's custodian, Robert Erwin. Thirtyish, I'd estimate, a great ox of a man yet amiably demeanoured, Erwin (brief after-work chats and the shared walk to the B-Line trolleys) would most often leave me uplifted via even his most stray comments. Many were the occasions when his simple positivities left me prickly with guilt, for here was a man who never had anything less than a smile to offer, even after having lost his wife to a malignancy, then one daughter to tuberculosis and a second to murderers. "You can be sure, Mr. Phillips," he regarded me once, "that every day I wake up, and the sun's still shinin' and the world's still turnin', and I've got a job when millions of others don't–*that's* a day to give thanks for. You see, Mr. Phillips, every day is a celebration . . ." The tenor of his voice left no denying his conviction, while most days I stewed in sentiments opposite, becoming poisoned now by my own misanthropy and self-inflicted gloom. We both lived in the district's west end—hence our sharing the B-Line. "Truly it's a great God that can see fit to shine His light on me," he said once. "You're a religious man, I take it?" came my dark question but he answered, "Not religious enough, but I don't s'pose anyone can be, not tainted as we are by Original Sin. All we can do is repent, right? We're all human bein's and we're all sinners. Yet God gives me my job and my beatin' heart, and you too! So I do my best to give Him my faith."

Such evangelical spouts I tried to avoid, yet something about his soft-spokeness, still, made me heed the words in spite of my resolute *dis*belief in his god. How could I, with my righteous sister likely dead?

But conversely . . . how could *he,* in all his tumultuous loss?

On the night in question Erwin and I chatted innocuously after-shift as we walked to the trolley-stop. Somewhere unseen an old iron-striker bell tolled four a.m., a plaintive, dismal sound. At this hour, as was usual, the ill-litten streets looked abandoned, and no rabble-rousers or "rummies," as they were called, were afoot, which always relieved me. A silence that seemed nervous, though, held dominion within the foetid air that hung between the leaning, rust-streaked edifices on either side. It had been a grueling shift, with my company's transcription quota rising to defray incremental costs. Erwin, likewise, had been passed over for a modest raise, for synonymous reasons. I couldn't help but poke some implied fun: "Could it be that your god's light isn't shining brightly as it once did?"

With a scoff, he replied, "Brighter! Are you kidding? Neither of us, Mr. Phillips, got cause to complain. Did you know that in Russia, they don't make but a nickel a day?"

I should've known! More of his positivity.

"But, you know," he continued, "I got to admit, maybe I didn't get that raise 'cos I'm bein' punished. God's way of reminding me who's boss."

"Punishment?" I questioned as we stood beneath a bleak town-gas lamp at the stop. "You're about as free of error as anyone I've met."

The pallored gas-light seemed to drain his ever-optimistic expression. "I can't be a hypocrite, Mr. Phillips. I've done my share'a sinnin'—always been sorry afterward, but still . . . Been thinkin' about it lately, to tell ya the truth."

I laughed aloud on the nighted, trash-strewn street. "Really, now? So if I may ask," I mocked, "what *grand sin* have you been contemplating?"

His seriousness, tinged by guilt, did not waver. "Sins of the flesh. What else?"

He must mean either salooning or whore-mongering, two activities I'd never partaken in. But I maintained my good-hearted chastisement. "Succumbing to the desires that your Creator gave you? Surely, Mr. Erwin, your god can't be so disingenuous as to refuse to forgive *that.*"

"Oh, He forgives it—the pastor says so—but only to those *worthy* of His forgiveness."

"And how on earth does one gauge *worthiness?*"

Suddenly, he looked lost. "I don't know."

But his words had me thinking, not his words of forgiveness from sin, but his *implications.* "So you mean you frequent the speakeasies, Mr. Erwin? The rot-gut some of those places pass off as illicit liquor can make one blind's what I've heard. Only days ago I read of one such den that served up devilish bad rum, and several died. There's that risk, compounded by the simple risk of being caught by violating the laws of the Eighteenth Amendment. Federal men are all over the city, I hear."

"Oh, I don't mean speakeasies, Mr. Phillips," and then he gulped. "Spirits are a vile polluter of the God-given human body. What I'm talking about . . . are the Red Houses . . ."

I nodded while keeping reins on my personal disapproval of such iniquitous havens. Though I recognised immorality when I saw it I was also thoughtful enough to refrain from judgments, and I could even compel myself to overlook Erwin's obvious hypocrisy: the stalwart Christian but one tainted by a weakness for ladies of the night. Of my own case, I'll say that so- called sexual congress caused me to harken back to the wise quip of Lord Halifax: "The price is damnable, the pleasure is momentary, and the position is ridiculous," which bespoke my views as well. I myself had thankfully never suffered from a high state of libidiny but I could hardly condemn others affected by more heightened—and notably *normal*—states. How was a good man such as Erwin expected to satisfy his natural primordial drives with a wife long dead? At last, I commented, "I must say, I can hardly picture a moral man as yourself frequenting such places."

"I can't say I frequent them, Mr. Phillips." He shifted his stance within the feeble shelter. "In fact, I've only been to one particular house ever, and only three times total."

It was not even a conscious thing that so grotesquely piqued my interest; it was the inundating pragmatism stoked instead by *unconscious* considerations. I was prepared to accept *any* circumstance that might lend credence to my hope that Selina was still alive. The unkindly booking sergeant's words creaked back like old ship timbers in my memory: *Lots 'a women have took to sellin' thereselfs, ya know* . . . Had such a demeaning fate been my sister's lot? Certainly she was well-figured enough to be viable for such a trade, her figure, yes, and most notably her bosom. I only hoped that this might actually be, for if it were, it meant that she'd still be among the living and, hence, retrievable.

A sudden surge in the coal-gas intensified the streetlamp's brightness, just as the idea had surged in my mind: *I could go to this brothel* . . . *and investigate* . . . Indeed, and not that I suspected Selina might work in this *particular* bordello but surely there stood a more-than-minute chance that some of the women therein had seen or even knew of her. I could show my picture around whilst maintaining the appearance of a "john," as I believed the suitors of prostitution were called.

For the first time in months, I had hope!

But, lo, even as the trove of my hope may have just trebled, simple realities proved another matter. Came my whisper, "I'd be interested in attending this 'Red House' with you, Mr. Erwin, but I'm afraid I've precious little money for such indulgences." My fingers fished through stray coins in my pocket. "How, uh, how much would be requisite on my part for, say, minimal services?"

Erwin's face loosened in a manner of relief. "Thank you for not disowning our friendship, Mr. Phillips. I thought sure you'd think me a cad for admitting this—"

"Not at all. We all have our occasions for urges oft beyond our force of will. But, hear me. How *much* will I need?"

He paused at the distant bay of a foghorn from the harbour, a seemingly unearthly dirge of murky, falling notes; but when it passed, he answered, "Well, the place I've been to, it's called the 1852 Club, and it's a strange place, I've got to say. You see—and you'll find this hard to believe—it's *free.*"

I eyed him in the wavering pallor of gas-light. "Did I hear you right? Free?"

"It's free, all right, Mr. Phillips," he assured in a whisper. "I been there three times, like I said, and haven't spent a penny."

How could I not scoff now? I argued, "That makes no sense whatever. Any commercial enterprise, licit or illicit, exists through the conduction of services or merchandise rendered in the exchange of some monetary source! A bordello that doesn't charge for the services of its women would be the uttermost negation of logic."

"You'll get no argument from me, Mr. Phillips," he maintained his whisper as if in fear of being overheard on the vacant street. "I'm just tellin' ya how it is. I know it sounds like a tall tale but . . . ," and then all he did was shrug.

A tall tale, yes, but I trusted in my judgment of men to be convinced that Erwin was no such teller. "Well," I said next. "Where exactly is this 1852 Club located?"

Erwin spread out his hands. "To tell you the truth, I'm not sure. Sometimes I think it must be near Old Greenwich and other times it seems it must be Lower East. It's the trolley that takes us, see—maybe a ten, fifteen-minute trip, but the *route . . .*"

"What about the route?" I insisted.

"It's all this way and that, and up and down, and through alleys I never seen before. It moves through these courtyards that look so *old,* and, and . . . Even a tunnel, where there's no light at all. Gettin' on by mistake one night's how I even found out about the place."

"That's very . . . strange," I uttered.

"Well like I first mentioned, it's a strange place." Suddenly he looked dreamy even in the smudged darkness. "The women, Mr. Phillips, it's just one looker after the next, and they don't wear nothin' about the house, I ain't kiddin' ya." His whisper grew heated. "And they do *anything,* and'll have ya as many times as you can go."

"All, as you ensure, for nothing," I reiterated.

"For nary a red cent."

By now the proposition seemed farcical, but I simply refused to believe Erwin would lie so cockamamily. "In that case, I'd like very much to join you tonight."

He seemed to shudder. "I just feel so . . . guilty, Mr. Phillips—"

"Oh, for goodness sake!" I complained. "*Guilty?*"

"It's hard enough staying on a Godly course, and I *do* try, but sometimes . . . sometimes—" He shook his head in remorse. "It's been more than six months since I've . . . well, you know . . ."

Six MONTHS? I thought all too stridently, *It's been more than six YEARS for me!*

Erwin composed himself out of his conflicting sentiments. "I only do it when I *have* to, but I see I've brought you right along into it. Not only are *my* sins on my hands but *your* sins, too."

I was losing patience now with the fulcrum on which Erwin's self-perceived "sin" teetered. But I *needed* him now. "I wouldn't worry about it, Erwin. Nature, just the same as your god, is what made us *men*, with the *natural proclivities* of men, so don't get yourself in a swiver. Now, when does the trolley come? Surely it's not the B-Line—"

"No, no. And it doesn't come every night, but when it does" —he consulted his pocket-watch with a squint— "it would be very soon." Another diverting pause cruxed his expression. "But that's another thing 'bout this place, Mr. Phillips, another *strange* thing, I mean." He stared off into drab darkness. "Time."

"*Time?*"

"I don't know how to explain it"—he rubbed his brows—"but each and every time I been, it's seemed like I been there for *hours*. I could get on with three or four different girls, too, and when I get out'a there I think it's got to be noon at least . . . but then I look at my watch and it's scarcely four-thirty in the morning or quarter till five."

I staved off a chuckle, for Erwin was permitting his oblique sense of abstraction to supervene the much more primal reality that he must not be possessed of much sexual endurance! Then again, how much endurance would *I* be capable of given the sheer infrequency of my own sexual experience? *Laughably little,* I suspected, for so long ago it was that'd I'd been married.

Several more minutes passed, and my current hopes passed as well. The B-Line would be arriving shortly. "Drat," I said. "It appears that tonight's not our night, Mr. Erwin," but no sooner had I spoken the words than Erwin turned with an enthused lurch . . .

At the end of the street, like something first semi-tangible slowly materializing from the dark's secret ether, a bulk shape began to form. Crackling sparks grew less dim (no doubt the sparks of electric transference from the ever-present power wires looping overhead), companioned by a faint and very ghostly circle of yellow light at the shape's forward-most area which made me think of a dying cyclopean eye. The squeal of bearings caught my ears, then the grate of an air-break . . .

Erwin uttered, "This is it."

The vehicle's forward lamp shined so faint it scarcely served a purpose, but finally there came another surge of gas into the closest street-lamp, and this is when I got my first full glimpse.

It was an older-style trolley, opened all around in a vestibuled fashion (in other words, lacking windows) and was of the antiquated twin-car, double-truck type whereas all city trolleys that I'd seen were single-carred. Flaking yellow paint, quite a murky yellow, covered all of the decrepit vehicle's side panels.

"This is most definitely *not* a city trolley," I muttered to Erwin.

"No, Mr. Phillips. It's a *private* trolley. It's not from the city transit system at all."

A *private* trolley . . .

At the forward car's head, I spied the motorman's station, little more than a cubby; the capped motorman himself stood scarcely moving at the controller handle. In the drear, his face looked deadpan, bereft of life; indeed, the darkness reduced his eyes and mouth to black slits amid a waxen pallor. Above the frame of his look-out, the car's identification number could be seen in black-stencil letters: *No. 1852.*

The vehicle squealed to a halt. Erwin, in an excitement that seemed touched by fear, grabbed my arm and urged, "The conductor'll size you up 'cos you're new, but don't worry. He'll let you on since you're with me."

"Size me up?" I had to question.

"They don't let ruffians on."

"Oh," but in a city *aswarm* with ruffians and every other manner of human flotsam, the policy was to be expected. "But who enforces order, should the conductor mistakenly allow some roysterers aboard?"

"The motorman," Erwin answered in a whisper tense with unpleasantness. "I seen it happen once. Hobos, all riled with liquor, jumped on and started a ruckus, but the ruckus didn't last long."

"The motorman's something of a tough customer, I take it."

Erwin looked troubled. "Let's just say that them hobos are probably *still* in the hospital."

Oh, my, I thought.

"Come on!"

The overhead cable sparked and crackled. I followed Erwin up the sheet-metal steps of the first car, and in doing so, I noticed other silent riders sitting among the wooden cross-seats; however, the wee hour's dimness reduced their faces to smears of shadow. The metal floor *tapped* at coming footfalls: the boots of the conductor, a short but sure-footed figure, who approached directly, eyed Erwin with a nod, and waved him aboard. "This here's my friend," Erwin softly informed. "Not a trouble-making bone in his body, I can vouch for it . . ."

The conductor, like the driver, wore a regulation cap and heavy, brass-buttoned jacket as was the fashion. He stared at me, or seemed to, for the car's irksome darkness forbade any details of his face, much in the same manner as the motorman. My skin crawled, however, in what I can only describe as a most abrupt accession of dread; for whatever unhealthful reason, I imagined I was being evaluated by either a mask of the most pallid parchment or the face of a dead man.

The moment locked in stasis.

"How do you do?" I bid with a bit of a stammer.

The conductor waved me aboard, then returned with lugubrious steps back to the vicinity of the motorman's station.

Sparks burst overhead in a brilliant blossom, and then the trolley lurched once and commenced down the nearly lightless street.

Erwin showed me the way down the aisle; carefully, we stepped over the heavy-iron coupling and passed into the rear car. "We've got to keep our voices down," came his incessant whisper. "That's why I brung us back here." I could hardly object; we both took seats at the car's rearmost section.

As I sat, I stared astonished into the grim, nighted city. The trolley clattered along the rusted rails to traverse unknown streets of ballast-cobble and past cramped lay-bys of various municipal departments that seemed long out of service. Was it my suspicious fancy or did each successive street-lamp put out less and less illumination? Brick facades and lichen-encrusted stone walls pressed ever inward; at one point we crossed what I believe was Amsterdam Avenue but as we did so, the sinister car rose to a clamour as the motorman increased speed, almost as if to pass through the dimly peopled intersection with as much haste as the motor would allow. Along this dismal way, we stopped on several occasions along similarly unfamiliar and quite ruinous corners to pick up additional passengers. As each boarder stepped up, he was assayed by the conductor for what I could only guess were traits of "approval": the smell of liquor on one's breath, loose talk, and perhaps even a subjective air of rowdiness would, of course, be disqualifiers. But as each man was allowed to come aboard, I noted quite readily that all possessed likewise bodily characteristics. These were all men of brawn and muscle, wide-shouldered, pillar-legged men of a solid working caste, much like Erwin. The only oddity to be admitted thus far was myself; with shoulders stooped, frail-bodied, and but 146 pounds, I hardly bore any commonality with these strong, ox-necked young men. (As a child, my mother perpetually referred to me as her "little waxbean." How complimentary . . .) But it was then the notion insinuated itself—in a manner I cannot explain by any substance— that the conductor was indeed "sizing up" potential visitors to the mysterious 1852 Club in hopes of selecting the most virile, the most sexually *potent* candidates. I couldn't imagine what might cause me to make such a conjecture. Two or three times, however, thinner and less-fecund-looking chaps were turned away. So . . .

Why on earth would a spindly-form such as myself be let aboard? Evidently the club held much stock in Mr. Erwin's credulity.

The car clattered onward for a time, then—

We were swallowed into darkness.

It was a musty, dripping tunnel we'd darted into, whose arched walls were eerily webbed by the faintest luminescent fungi. When I turned to look Erwin full in the face, I could make no trace of him. Ahead, in the forward car, did a passenger gasp in sudden startlement?

"I told ya, Mr. Phillips. There be a tunnel or two." He chuckled nervously. "Hope you're not one to be afraid of the dark."

"I daresay even a man of the stoutest heart might be timid in darkness this complete," said I, looking around but seeing essentially nothing save for the foxfire-like etchings. "This is a queer trek indeed."

"It's worth it, though." He tugged my sleeve just to give me a bearing. "Remember what I said—the women are *lookers*."

"Yes," I grated.

"Best-looking one of 'em all is the madam—Miss Aheb— though she don't, you know, turn a trick herself. I only seen her once but . . . her *body* . . . It's enough to make a man bay at the moon."

A cruel trust on my part but I couldn't help but rib my "Christian" friend about his continuing hypocrisy. "By perfect, I'm certain you mean that all that God creates is perfect and therefore exists in a totality of beauty, eh, Erwin? You couldn't even remotely be founding your observation upon the venal sin of lust . . ."

Erwin said nothing in response, until I assured him I was joking. "Very funny, Mr. Phillips."

I chuckled over several rude bumps in the rail. "But, excuse me, Erwin, did you say the 'madam' of the club goes by the name of *Aheb?*"

"Yes, a furren name, I s'pose."

Furren? I pondered, then, *Ah, he means foreign.* "It's actually Egyptian and . . ." I paused in the clattering dark. "Almost sinister . . ."

I could sense him peering at me. "Sinister? You should *see* her, man. Ain't nothin' sinister about her. She's *beautiful.*"

"So you've said. It's simply the name," I related. "As you know, I was once a professor of history, but my most refined field of study was that of secret ancient mythologies. I'm referring to the mythological queen of a pre-dynastic Egyptian culture known as the Ahebites whose cryptic ruler was a notorious witch-priestess called Isimah el-*Aheb.* We're talking circa 5000 B.C., Erwin, which pre-dates the first official hieroglyphs by over fifteen hundred years. The story of Aheb, though very obscure, was similar to the mythologies of ancient Greece—Homer's *Iliad,* for instance, or the legends of Zeus and Poseidon—only rather than portraying the conquest of good over evil, we find quite the opposite—*fictions,* I mean, written either to entertain or to fabulise the inception of humankind." I raised my finger in utter dark. "Ah, but there are always those who attest that certain fables aren't fables at all, but *fact.*"

This, of course, I in no way believed, but the mythology at large was one that had long held my interest. Whose interest it was *not* holding, however, was that of Erwin, who merely replied to my dissertation with an unemphatic "Oh, uh, really?"

I needed to put the pedantry of my bygone university days behind me; after all, I was a man on his way to a whore-house. Common working folk such as Erwin would not be roused in the least by such an arcane mythos. It was merely curious, though, the name of this "madam": Aheb. How could it *not* cause me to reflect upon those fascinating older-than-ancient myths which detailed the supernatural revel of the Ahebites and their sacrificial reverence to an immense commune of limbless gods hailed as the Pyramidiles? These hideous deities existed as but pallid hulks of flesh, never moving, only thinking, only *perceiving.* The Pyramidiles, yes. Their human agent upon the earth was the obscene sorceress Isimah el-Aheb who had enspelled her people to bow down to these revolting cosmic abominations, paying homage to their nether-dimensional *bulk* by way of enfrenzied orgies and ravenous blood-baths which in turn generated the psychical horror on which these gods so thrived; indeed, it was the carnally beauteous el-Aheb who orchestrated rampant earthly horror in veneration; and to whom the Pyramidiles had blasphemously blessed with the gift of immortality via the sickish mold-green tincture that was but one of their wicked secrets. To her also they'd whispered their arcane manner of writing: a form of gematria, the substitution of numbers for letters. Once learned of all the Pyramidiles' harrowing secrets, el-Aheb ruled the ancient outlands, to slaughter, pillage, rape, and defile, all in the name of the Pyramidiles, who lived on realms not of this earth or even this solar system, but in the screaming upside-down crevices between space and time; indeed, the Pyramidiles, the Putrid-Flesh Gods; eyeless, brain-filled masses of otherworldly *organa,* each the size of a mountain and, suspiciously, the shape of a *pyramid . . .*

What an intriguing and ultimately macabre old legend!

With more iron clatter and a swoosh, the previously unrelieved darkness broke—much to my commendation—as Trolley No. 1852 at last exited the deleterious tunnel and now roved down more dim, tenement-lined streets. Looking behind me, I noted that the overhead power-cables were no longer in evidence, and we seemed to be traveling along railways so long out of use that their heavy wooden ledgers had gone to rot. I could only assume that batteries now provided the trolley its propulsion, for how else could this be without the connexion of the overhead electricity cables?

"Almost there," Erwin whispered.

Through more stone archways the sullen car delved; archways in the most decrepit brick walls; block-rimmed *maws* agape and garlanded by sickly ivy. Next, we crept through a series of grotesque yet captivating courtyards of what could only be abandoned edifices, each bizarrely interconnected by narrower archways. This was the old city, no doubt, one of several urban nooks left to disrepair and rendered tenantless via the contagion of outside squalor and ruination; truly we were traveling amid the very bowels of New York. Grainy wedges of moonlight cast a feeble pallor over all as broken statues watched the trolley from neglected sconces and rats scurried about fieldstone tiles and garbage-filled fountain basins. But it was in one of these eldritch inner-courtyards that the trolley suddenly slowed, jostled, then squealed to a stop . . .

I looked about, nearly at a loss for words. This courtyard stood in no less disintegration than the others: festooned by ivy, verminous with weeds. Rotten fabrics hung from the stone rails of second-, third-, and fourth-story verandas, while numerous once-fine marble statues stood armless, headless, and stained by lichens and bird-waste.

"What *is* this place, Erwin?" I whispered.

"This is it," he told me. "Don't be fooled by how it looks outside; I think they do it on purpose."

I could only imagine he meant a deliberate subterfuge was at hand, to throw off suspicions of the uninvited, for who would think that any desirous activity could possibly take place behind so unkempt and dismal a facade?

Erwin and I were the last in line as the passengers all stood up to file in utter silence off the car. When I happened a glance to my pocket-watch, I saw that it was 4:12 a.m. As the queue moved down the aisle, however, I took notice, first, of the trolley's position; it had stopped mid-yard, yet the rusted tracks continued forward to disappear beneath a great iron-beamed and rivet-studded door set solidly within yet another wide stone arch. Was it the shifting moonlight or my strained imagination that made me believe I saw traces of an oily, ill-coloured mist leaking through the door's seams? What I noticed next must've been still another trick of poor-light: my glimpse forward, past the slowly descending line of debarking passengers, threw my gaze onto the motionless form of the motorman, who remained in his piloting cubby, his broad back to us, and his hand on the vehicle's controller handle—his *hand,* I say . . .

My stomach knotted.

His hand, though I only glimpsed it for a moment, appeared as no hand at all but a cluster of rather stout worms wrapped about the controller handle's end. Just as disturbing as the morphology of the hand was its *colour:* a bloodless white splotched with ill-toned green . . .

When a stiff chill passed, I realised it must either be dirtied utility gloves or some regrettable genetic malady.

The line dwindled; before I stepped off, my gaze felt preternaturally summoned to my left. There I spied the capped conductor staring right at me through the mask-like deadpan facial expression . . .

Gads!

I deboarded in haste and hurried up to Erwin who was following the others in. A rotten, wood-plank sign hung upon the transom of worm-eaten but iron-strapped door. The letters on the sign appeared branded in char: *1852 Club.*

Torches, not electric bulbs, lit an expansive and ornately decor'd atrium which borrowed much from the greater Georgian period; clearly, this place must once have been an exorbitant hotel. Swirling dark mosaic tile-work could be seen in the gaps between Old World throw rugs; a marble fountain gushed crystalline water through the mouth of a horned cherub. Pilastered walls surrounded all; while great winding staircases rose upward from each end, to the first of three splendidly railed stair-halls which steeply overlooked the atrium below.

I allowed Erwin to take the lead; he and most of the others seemed nearly at home here, and all walked at once to a long, fringe-linened banquet table which sat heaped with fresh fruits and (much to *my* displeasure) ice-filled bins loaded with half-shelled oysters. It was to the latter that most of the men repaired, greedily slurping down the hideous, lumpen things one after another. As I most infrangibly *detested* all shellfish—most especially oysters, which made me think of grey phlegm—I made every attempt to appear at ease while sampling some tidbits of fruits and a glass of some superb vegetable juice. Eventually to Erwin I whispered, "So . . . where are the, uh—"

"The girls? Before you know it," he promised with a guilty grin, "they'll be all about."

Only moments after he'd made this assurance, every face turned upward at the detection of svelte motion. Upon the fourth stair-hall my gaze held, on the stunning woman who'd just appeared: a raven-haired, Cleopatra-faced figure whose voluptuous curves and thrusting bosom were made even more pronounced by a diaphanous, black evening dress.

"That's her," Erwin sighed in awe. "Miss Aheb . . ."

Ensconced torches burned to either side as this shimmering *vision* of feminine beauty leaned over the carven rail and smiled.

"Welcome, gentlemen, all of you," issued a lilting and vaguely accented voice. The words echoed. "Your presence is much appreciated and, as you will soon see, the very exclusive 1852 Club will do everything in its power to reward you for the privilege your esteemed presence . . ."

What an odd thing to announce . . . as denotations such as "esteemed" and "privileged" hardly described this lot of respectful yet otherwise brawny and likely not-well-educated working-classers.

I struggled to identify the seductive woman's sweetly flowing accent; yet I'll admit that the mere sight of her compacted beauty filched my breath. There was something about her mien, her very *deportment.* Even at this precipitous distance, her physique's details seemed to gleam via some supernal clarity, as though an incorporeal magnifier hung invisibly before her: the poreless white valley of her bosom, the relief of the papillae of her magnificent breasts, the diamond-like sparkle of perfect teeth within the titillant smile—*all* of these traits seemed amalgamated into a single focus which left every man below speechless and irretrievably enraptured.

Erwin elbowed me. "What did I tell you, huh?"

"I'll confess," I said, still staring up, "that I dismissed your description earlier as the stuff of exaggeration, but now . . . I stand corrected."

Her voice swirled downward, a spiriferous aural wraith; and from the painfully seductrene lips, warm words flowed, "and, now, my good and vital men, may you go forth in the natural pursuit of your pleasure as is the gracious will of our benefactors . . ."

The room hushed in the lovely echo's wake but I frowned. Even the clearly distracted Erwin seemed flummoxed by the words.

"What d'ya s'pose she means by that?" Erwin said in a wee voice.

Benefactors? I wondered. "You've got me. 'Natural pursuit' notwithstanding, I sorely doubt that her reference to 'benefactors' can be a spiritual reference, nor a reference to the popular Judeo-Christian God, no, not in a whorehouse."

I paused to chuckle at my ever-guilt-ridden friend but when I re-glanced upward?

Miss Aheb was gone.

A modest murmuring of approval rose in the room—at once—as a procession of over a dozen women moved soft-footedly down the curved, plushly carpeted staircase. I've already intimated that my own natural impulses with regard to sexual attraction must be relatively inactive compared to most men; yet, the registration of this drove of encroaching sprites (all without a stitch on, mind you) caused an undeniable stirring, shall we say, southwardly of the belt. The well-brawned patronage was already dispersing as this bevy of long-legged, high-bosomed, and pertly nippled women came off the stairs.

Erwin, a smile so long it contorted his face, made to approach them but I clutched his sleeve in a sudden self-consciousness.

"Gads, Erwin! I've never been to a place like this before. What should I do?"

The question flabbergasted him. "Do? Come on! You pick a dish and go with her, man!" and then he walked briskly to the feminine congregation and its sea of wanton grins. I remained, standing nervously and watching couples pair off. The girls seemed to swoop upon the men with a hearty enthusiasm; but, lo, none "swooped" toward me. Never much of a ladies' man, I expected as much; these younger and much more masculine specimens easily overshadowed my thin-limbed form. I would always tell myself that what manly attributes nature had left me lacking in was more than made up for in my superior intellectual capacity, but what a facile consolation that was now! In a whorehouse, with no whore showing the least bit of interest in me! Erwin was latched onto and led summarily up the stairs by a doe-eyed, plushly curved girl with a head full of shining black tousles. *Good for you,* I thought with some bitterness. Within the merest of minutes, the men were arm in arm with each of these delectable women whose bare bottoms I was left to peer forlornly at as they each in turn took their partners up the steps. I felt akin to the perfect ass, but just as it seemed that all the denuded girls had found their match, my arm was snatched by a short, voracious thing with beaming green eyes and nary an ounce of excess fat on her splendid little body. "I've got you now!" she exclaimed and quickly hauled me toward the stairs. "My name's Ammi, but don't bother telling me yours. In a place like this?" and she laughed.

The sight of her, and the feel of her hot hand about my wrist, left my tongue sufficiently tied. Instead, my eyes drunk up the vision of her gleaming white nudity; the compact buttocks flexing with each step up; the seductively trim waist and adorable bellybutton. Already my groin was tightening . . .

"Don't talk much, I see," she commented and now we were on the first landing where a statue of, I believe, Tycho Brahe, telescope in hand, seemed to cast an approving eye my way. "But we're not much about talk here at the club—" Her hand slid up my arm. "We're all about *doing*."

Finally, my powers of speech were re-afforded to me. "You're, uh, quite a delight, Ammi. I, um—"

Her hand brazenly cradled my rump as we stepped up to the second landing. "Oh, don't be so nervous. I'm going to show you a great time!"

Patrons ahead of us disappeared behind various doors. Ammi took me sprightly along the carpeted hall, almost *bounding* with each step. She approached a door and simultaneously slid her hand across my groin, whereupon I came close to lifting off my heels.

She paused at the door, turning to me with a scolding grin. "Shame on you, sir. There's no reason to do *that*, you know. Not *here!*"

It was only then, receiving my first frontal look at her, that I became apprised of the extent of Ammi's *diversity*. To call her a "colourful" girl would be a howling understatement: her hair was a long silken coppery red while obsidian-black eyebrows adorned her forehead. The abundant hair of her pubic area, however, shined blond as sunlit wheat. Breasts the circumference of tangerines sat erect on her chest. Only after fathoming this full glance at her did I recollect her odd remark.

"Pardon me, but I don't know what you mean. There's no reason to do *what?*"

Her hand found my groin again, and played there ever intently. "This *package*, sir, can't all be you," she giggled. "Oh, I know how men sometimes stuff socks and whatnot in their briefs to make themselves look bigger to the ladies but—really!—in a brothel, sir, the truth is always out once the breeches are down."

I stared in utter bewilderment. "*Socks,* did you say? Really, miss—I can't imagine what—"

"Come on!" she exclaimed, opened the door, and pulled me in.

The door itself was a marvel: nine panels, and hung within a stunning embrasured frame that I knew at a glance to be pure Federal Period. The bed-chamber impressed me even more, as I'd always been one to revel in the designs of the past rather than those of tasteless modernity. "A genuine William and Mary poster bed!" I gasped. The black-oak bedstead was a work of carven art. A Chippendale half-table sat beside the splendid bed, while opposite stood a grand armoire that could only be a genuine Hepplewhite. My host's delightful breasts bobbed as she closed the door, then strode toward me. She grabbed my hand and pulled, and said as if to a naughty toddler, "You're a *bad boy,* sir. Ammi might have to punish you with a spanking for what you've done."

She grabbed an exquisite steamed-wood chair about and plopped right down in it, positioning me to stand before her.

"I say, you'd be advised to treat that chair with care, miss," I warned. "Unless I'm mistaken, it's a genuine Adam. The canework alone is without peer."

"Oh, shut *up,* you," she sputtered and at once fumbled with my belt. "We'll get to the bottom of *this.* If it's all you in here, I'll be a monkey's aunt . . ."

I remained mystified by her coy complaint. A sudden modesty overwhelmed me when she unfastened my trousers, then hastily slid them down along with my briefs.

Ammi stared with a dropped jaw, stared right at my bared groin. "You've *got* to be kidding me . . ."

"What?" I asked, but my feet shifted a bit, from the cringing embarrassment of being so closely and privately examined. All I could think to utter was, "I, uh, I suppose it's not as large as you're use to," and I chuckled nervously "But there's little I can do about *that.*"

She gaped up with jade-green irises burning beneath the blacker-than-onyx eyebrows. "Not as *large?* This is the biggest prick I've ever *seen . . .*"

Her remark befogged me, for in her tone I detected not a trace of prevarication. "You, uh, you mean to say that my . . . member is more sizable than the average you're accustomed to?"

She snapped in a course delight. "It's the biggest *cock* I've ever had hanging in my face, and I can tell you, there've been quite a few!" and with that she began to stroke the drooping shaft of flesh with a lithe finger.

I chuckled. "You flatter me, Ammi, but I'm sure you're being over-lenient in your assessment of my privates."

She giggled another "Shut *up!*" and without reservation sucked the entirety of my flaccid penis into her mouth. The adroitness of her oral skill sent shivers through my being. (This, for me, was a pleasure long forgotten; my ex-wife had a knack for it, I will say, but her preference for penetration always won out. Many was the night I'd gaze at the ceiling contemplating Poe, Machen, and Blackwood whilst she hopped ludicrously up and down on me, enfrenzied akin to a mare in heat.) But as for this highly spirited and deliciously naked Ammi, erecting my manhood seemed to be her most steadfast desire. It didn't take long before its girth actually stretched her lips. She nearly gagged sliding it out. "Jesus *Christ*, mister! It's so big I can't even get it all in my mouth!"

"I—I . . . don't know what to say . . ."

She checked my hands, examining them, evidently, for traces of a wedding band. "So you're *not* married?"

"Oh, no, not anymore."

"Well, it's an awful shame that some happy woman isn't getting *this* stuck in her every night!"

I felt foolish presuming to converse whilst my nearly erect privates wobbled up and down, and that was not to mention the *preposterous* entails of our discourse. "I was married once but I'm afraid the halls of academe proved far more my forte than the pastures of domesticity and wedlock."

She glared at me. "Shut *up!*" and then she yanked me to the bed and nearly threw me down on it. "Now . . . I've just *got* to know!"

I peered toward where she now rummaged through a drawer in the spectacular armoire. "Know what, if I may ask?"

"Just how *big* this monster is!" she replied, returning with a tin ruler. Her frenzied hand pumped the penile shaft in utter awe, until full erection had been achieved, whereupon she aligned the rule to it . . .

"Holy *shit!*" she profaned.

My penis, now fully invigorated, slightly exceeded the rule's maximum length.

It was a twelve-inch rule.

Ammi went all in a frenzy now, retrieving something else from the armoire and then returning to the bed to boldly straddle me with her bare hips. "No more fooling around," she determined, opening a modest foil package. "For every minute that this gorgeous cock isn't buried in my bush, that's a minute of *horrible* waste!"

"What's that . . . you've got there?" I asked, my eyes asquint.

"Don't want to put a bun in little Ammi's oven, do you?"

The frail, flavescent object in her hands was a barrier prophylactic, one of the newer Latex versions by its look. I could hardly object to its non-prescriptive and, hence, *illegal* utility here, as prostitution was no *less* illegal.

Ammi's face turned flustered, and, again, she profaned, "Shit, your cock's so big, I hope it doesn't *bust* the goddamn thing!"

My frown was all-too quick. "Ammi, if I may? Profanity does your demeanour *precious little* justice."

She squinted at me. "The *fuck?*" and then she carefully rolled the prophylactic all the way down my penile shaft.

"*Now* we're talkin'," she gasped with a smile after essentially sitting on my erection and licensing it full entry into her womanly channel. "God–yeah, oh, *fuck* that's good . . . *All* the way in, yeah! *All* the way in!"

The sensations were admittedly quite pleasing but I'm afraid Ammi's vandalism of the English language and her crude, splayed-legged pelvic locomotions left much to be desired. At one point she reached behind herself and cosseted my scrotal sack, only to further profane, "For fuck's sake, mister. Even your *balls* are huge! They feel like something in the goddamned *hen house!*"

Indeed.

Her copulative motions accelerated, hands on knees as she continued to *pound* her loins upon my phallus. As she tended to the act, I, instead, surveyed more of the room's splendid features. The elaborate wainscoting was absolutely fabulous (more of the Georgian Period) while the wall-coverings couldn't have pleased me more: herringbone patterns of gold and vermillion. When I craned my neck to examine a considerable oil landscape on the wall, I had to request, "Pardon me, Ammi, but would you know if that formidable painting there is an original Turner? It seems to be."

Her lust-pinkened face smoldered. "Shut *up!* We're doing *this* now! *This! Shit* on the goddamn painting!" Sweat beaded on her face and misted her bosom. "With my luck you'll be one of these guys who gets off in a minute . . ."

Hmmm, I considered.

In not one but *twenty minutes'* time, Ammi was balloon-cheeked and shrieking in an undisputable ecstatic bliss. The purse of her womanhood spasmed desperately about the stiff meat of my sexual organ; I dare say, it seemed to squirm in time with her rising shrieks. When she'd had her protracted moment, her head wobbled on her neck, and she sidled over on the priceless bed, tongue hanging. Fast-breath'd, she grinned lazily. "That was the best fuck of my life . . .," and after a few more moments of recapturing her wind, she manipulated herself around, to look flabbergasted at my still-stiff-as-a-baker's-pin penis.

"Did you come?"

I elevated a brow. "If by that you mean did I experience an ejaculatory release and sequent orgasm? No."

"Wait right there!" she exclaimed and abruptly roused. She stalked, if a bit painfully, toward the ornate door but stopped to point absurdly at my erected member. "And don't let *that* go away!"

Oh, for goodness sake! Where did she expect my penis to go? After she'd made her exit, I felt *ridiculous* lying there with my trousers down and a rubber-sheathed erection throbbing. Where could she be off to?

And I mustn't forget to show her Selina's photo . . .

Ammi's return brought four more women into the room: two svelte blondes, a lissome brunette, and a fox-eyed coif-headed waif with raving auburn hair and a *monumental* mammarian endowment.

"Good *God!*" one croaked, eyeing me.

"She wasn't lying!" excited another.

The auburn-head seemed locked in a rigor. "Is that . . . *real?*"

It was one of the blondes that lunged before the others and asserted, "This guy may be able to out-fuck Ammi, but he ain't gonna out-fuck *me,* and that's just as sure as pigs can *shit!*"

The language absolutely *appalled* me.

It was a rather monotonous foray which ensued; four more giddy naked women clucking over my genitals like great-grandams over knickknacks. One by one they punctured themselves on my stiffened-to-numbness erection, shrilly giggling in betwixt moans, gasps, and outright shrieks of lascivious liberation. Musky aromas swam about the chamber, accompanied by a rapid, wet *clicking;* sweating bellies sucked inward and out; eyes rolled up in sockets and tongues jutted; crystalline sweat dripped off tumid nipples. They rode me like some brute beast of sexual burden (which reminded me, quite regrettably, of my ex-wife). It was that second blonde, ostensibly the dominant of the five, who banged my penis to the proverbial hilt in a screaming, staccato madness fit for some carnal chasm in Dore's *Inferno,* and after achieving a head-whipping crisis, she leeringly lifted her pelvis off my member and without abatement, then, inserted said member into what I can only think to describe as a more *netherly* orifice.

"Right up my butt now, Mr. Big Dick," she guttered. "Just the way I *like* it!"

It unnerved me, needless to say, to know that I had been hoodwinked into performing the forbidden and historically blasphemous act so named for the ancient city of iniquity, Sodom. The sluttish woman's squat strained wider, affording me an all-too-precise view; and the ease with which she was able to admit the full depth and width of my member into this alternate and most uncomely cavity left me to conjecture that she was hardly a stranger to the act. She chuckled at my gape, then pressed two fingers to either side of her clitoral bulb, to isolate the mysterious nerve cluster. I visibly gulped, noting its size: nearly that of an avocado pit!

"Ammi likes to eat a box," she grated, "so she can get her little fuck-face over here and eat *this* one!" whereupon she grabbed the wickedly grinning Ammi by a crude fistful of coppery hair and shoved her face into the tensely splayed crotch. Ammi's mouth squandered no time whatever in ministering as directed. The activity begat a sound like an animal nursing.

"Fuck!" the blonde grunted. "This guy's tallywhacker is so big it's punching my goddamn *stomach!*"

All the girls shrieked laughter at the remark.

Between the sensation of my organ buried in her bowel and that of Ammi's tending oration, the blonde soon became a veritable dervish of flesh as once again she clenched and shivered, and then was wracked by another clearly thoroughgoing orgasmic salvo. And though I'll admit that the much more precise purchase of the act of sodomy rendered some pleasing sensations to myself, I was now quite lost in an unfathomable ennui. Women could be so *silly* sometimes, could they not? I forced my mind to focus on the task of letting nature, however contorted, take its course, and was grateful to then deliver the viscid proof of my own crisis into the prophylactic.

Finally!

"Fuck," the blonde moaned only to sidle over as if narcolyzed. Ammi giggled, wiping her sheened mouth. "Mister," she said to me, "you just fucked five *whores* to kingdom come!"

The remark, which I supposed was a compliment, left me inwardly very weary. "Well, Ammi, ladies. That was, uh, quite nice but I think I'll bid my adieu now and repair to the atrium." I frowned at the sullied condom on my now-slackening penis. "But I'd best get rid of this thing first . . ."

I prepared to remove the vulgar sheath, but then Ammi reached forward, strangely as if in alarm. "No, no!" she shrilled. "I'll take care of that! After all, it's, uh . . . it's my job," and with *that* curious comment, she gingerly removed the soiled vulcanized barrier.

Then, even more curiously, she held the thing out, suspended from her fingertips, for all to see, and in an excited squeal, said, "Girls! Look at this!"

The four other docile women looked at the unrolled object in what seemed absolute astonishment.

"Can you *believe* all that *jism?*"

Indeed, my expended seed was quite milkily obvious as it depended at the prophylactic's tip, though I couldn't imagine what the fuss was about. *What else would these silly girls expect?* I wondered.

"That's a *lot* of nut!"

"Shit. Looks like enough cum for *half a dozen* guys . . ."

"Mr. Big Dick is a walking creamery!"

Ammi chuckled her way out of the room, carrying with her the ridiculous sheath of latex. But in all this ballyhoo, and in spite of the undeniable attractiveness of my coarse-mouthed companions, I'd simply had enough. Ah, but I couldn't leave just yet, could I?

"Ladies, if I may impose upon you a moment?" I requested and showed them the photograph of my only sibling. "This is my sister, Selina Phillips, and I'm most dire to locate her. Might any of you have seen her about anywhere?"

The question set my heart to racing!

The naked and quite exhausted quattro all squinted at the photo, registered blank expressions, then shook their heads no.

Drat! All that tomfoolery for nothing!

I mumbled specious niceties in my departure, and bound for the door . . .

"'Bye, Mr. Big Dick!'"

"Yeah! 'Bye!"

"There goes the cream-wagon!"

"Come back again, please!"

I didn't waste my breath in informing them that such a prospect presented a very *low* order of probability . . .

Whew! I thought once back on the stair-hall and finally away from the dizzy cluster of trollops. More trollops (and likely just as dizzy) would have to be sought out and questioned about Selina; for the moment, though, I desperately needed a breather.

Past the stair-hall rail I noticed a spectacular hanging candelabrum; from there, I looked down and saw several male patrons loitering about the banquet table, most seeming to slurp down more of the loathsome oysters. These men had obviously finished their first sexual assignations and were affording themselves a break before pursuing another. There was no sign, however, of my associate Mr. Erwin.

A shrill rabble of feminine bombast resounded at the hall's end, where I spied Ammi's bare form proudly displaying the depending condom to another nude sprite—a pointy-breasted brunette. "Holy *cow!*" exclaimed the latter one eyeing the semen-filled reservoir. "*Look* at it all!"

"I know," gushed Ammi, "can you believe it? And the guy fucked the daylights out of all of us!"

"Holy *cow!*"

Great Pegana, I thought dismally. Could I help it that my seminal deposits were evidently much more voluminous than the average?

"And you should've seen his goddamn prong! Big as a baby's leg, I swear—he fucked me so hard I'll be walking like a cowboy for a *week!*"

I hid behind a somewhat Doric display pedestal, so not to be seen; what I needed less than anything just then was this pointy-breasted one wanting to sample my wares, too.

"I better get this upstairs," Ammi said, more quietly, of the ludicrous condom. "You already take yours?"

"Yeah, two so far . . ."

I felt my brow furrow at the arcane discourse. *They're clearly talking about . . . spent prophylactics. How eccentric . . .*

The elfin pair separated, Ammi moving up the stairs to the fourth story—or I'd be more accurate to say *limping.*

At that same moment a door farther down clicked open and out stepped another brazenly unattired prostitute—this one with nipples sticking out like persimmons—only to turn down the stairs and proceed behind Ammi. But this woman, too, had a spent prophylactic dangling from her fingers!

And a moment later?

A third woman did the same . . .

My astonishment was plain. *What cryptic onus could POSSIBLY charge these petite strumpets with the task of carrying away used prophylactics UPSTAIRS?* Surely, the nearest waste basket would do . . .

The hall remained clear, but when I emerged from my hiding, my eyes inadvertently fixed on the previously unnoticed object sitting atop the display pedestal: a crude beige cylindrical clay-shape roughly the size of a common pail; when recognition alighted, I muttered beneath my breath a shopworn, "Oh my God!" for I knew all too well what the unlikely object was:

A *cuneiform* cylinder.

As any archaeologist and, indeed, professor of ancient histories would know, these objects provided humankind with its very first "books," the most famous example being the Cyrus Cylinder which, in intricate cuneiform, detailed the conquest of Babylon by the Persian warrior Cyrus the Great and verified the prophet Isaiah's prediction in Old Testament papyri scrolls of the same two centuries previous. *This* cylinder, however (as, I add, without meaning to brag, that I am well-versed in many variations of cuneiform) did not bear the typical assortments of logograms, pictoglyphs, and polyphonous sequences of wedges and slants that the early writing system is known for. Instead, the clay cylinder before me was covered entirely with the exclusive stylus marks used to denote *numbers.*

The entire cylinder, I reiterate, had been so inscribed.

Oh, if I only had a month's time to decipher this cylinder, I lamented.

I let my considerations stew, along with my adjacent perplexity regarding the mysterious redeposition of expended condoms to some paradoxical upward recess of the building. I knew I must not make myself obvious; therefore, I strolled about the stair-hall half-pretending to examine various statues, paintings, and other pedestalled *objets-d'art.* Periodically, however, I took hasty opportunities to put my ear to each invaluable nine-paneled door I passed . . .

"Ooo-ooo-ahh-ahh . . . oh, YES!"

"Churn me like butter, honey!"

"Good, good! That's a *good* boy!"

All of the shrill exclamations were in feminine tones and clearly indicative of some manner of fornication.

The hall quieted, then, in seeming increments; alternately, the doors I'd just quitted opened to release, first, a brawny man with a sated smile on his face, and then his corresponding fornicatress.

Each naked woman, as I might've suspected by now, dispatched at once from the room to the stairs, and *up*. And from the fingertips of each suspended a spent prophylactic.

The bizarreness of my observations were by now getting the best of me. Clearly, more rooms existed upstairs on the fourth floor, yet not one prostitute had taken a man thither; which left me to deliberate: *The only person I know for fact to be up there is the club's madam . . . Miss Aheb . . .*

Could it be to Miss Aheb *that these shapely, bouncing-breasted "slatternettes" were delivering the epigrammatic soiled condoms?*

And if so . . .

Why?

I hadn't a notion. Eventually I repaired back to the exorbitant atrium where I found my friend Erwin (looking a bit dogged) helping himself to some refreshment. His grin greeted my arrival. "This place is something, huh, Mr. Phillips?"

"Something . . . yes," I uttered.

"The girl I got was pure dynamite, and she was none-too-disappointed with my performance, if ya don't mind me sayin' so."

"Not at all," I told him distractedly.

"Which girl did you get?"

I nearly moaned. *If you mean which FIVE GIRLS did I GET, I couldn't begin to tell you.* I simplified the response by merely saying, "A more-than-satisfactory little hussy by the name of Ammi, quite uniquely possessed of various hair colours."

"Don't know what mine's name was but I can tell you, she's quite good at putting more than food in her mouth."

"A laudable endorsement, indeed," I chuckled. I leaned over to keep my whisper more discrete. "But allow me to ask, and I apologize for the crudity, but . . . did your partner, um, make off with the soiled condom once the business was done?"

"Matter'a fact she did, Mr. Phillips, and now that'cha mention it? They always do."

"Doesn't that strike you as singularly peculiar?"

He stroked his stubble-blued chin. "Yeah, it does. Ya'd think they'd just drop it in the room's waste can but maybe they dispose of 'em all in the same place, as a safety precaution."

I squinted at his conclusion. "I'm afraid I'm not comprehending you, Mr. Erwin."

"Well, any red house is always leery of a raid. If the coppers broke in and found used skins in every room, it'd be a snap to get a prosecution, wouldn't ya think?"

"Why, I hadn't thought of that," I confessed, and I admitted, too, that in the remotest sense it did make some juris-prudential sense. But . . .

Somehow, however abstractedly, I couldn't quite fathom the notion to any sufficient degree of acceptability.

"I'll be going back for seconds, Mr. Phillips. You?"

"Oh, indeed," I transfigured the truth. More sexual frolic was most definitely *not* my preference, but I thought it best to obfuscate the truth to maintain more the air of a "team player." I did very much need to screen more of the working girls, to show them Selina's photograph.

Erwin seemed suddenly frustrated. "That is if there're any girls left I could grab seconds with. You heard the rumor, Mr. Phillips?"

"Rumor? Why, no."

"Heard two girls yacking about it a minute ago. Apparently one of the men was with us on the trolley is *quite* the stud. They say he took care'a *five girls* in one go-round and wore 'em completely out. They won't be hob-knobbin' with no one the rest'a the night. They also said the fella had something 'tween his legs that should'a been hangin' in the smokehouse." He elbowed me with a wink and a smile. "That fella wouldn't be *you*, now would it, Mr. Phillips?"

I let out a strapping laugh. "Only in my most delusory dreams!"

"Well—" He theatrically dusted off his hands. "I'm ready as I'll ever be . . . and may God forgive me."

I rolled my eyes and laughed.

"You coming up too?"

"I'll be along presently," was my erroneous response.

Erwin embarked for the stairs, in his search for "seconds."

The other refractors, as I'd come to think of them, had also returned upwards in the same search, leaving me the atrium to myself. At once, I contemplated my next tactic; any women who might recognise Selina's photo would be upstairs as well, on the second or third story. However . . .

An echoic click came to my ears, that elevated my gaze.

The conductor, I thought.

For there he was, the regulation cap perched atop the macabrely immobile white face. In the fashion of an automaton, he took slow steps up the winding stairs—to the *fourth* story . . .

Though my tactic remained undelineated, it was my sheer curiosity that overrode any action of greater utility.

You see, I *had* to know: exactly *what* was taking place on the ominous *fourth* story.

I gave the conductor only enough lead-time to conceal my movements; then, with stealth, speed, and deliberation, I traced his identical steps. Upon the fourth-floor landing, I hid behind another Doric display pedestal; this one providing the base for an ancient basalt idol whom I believed to be the notorious demon Baalzephon so actively worshiped by luciferic sects of the Middle Ages. Eye lined up along the pedestal's edge, I watched the conductor propel himself to the center of the grandiose stair-hall, pause, and then enter a door.

Now's my chance, I realised.

No one else occupied the hall, so I made haste across the plush carpeting. But my dilemma was plain; for although more than half a dozen doors lined the wall-side of the hall, I could not be certain exactly *which* door the blanch-faced man had entered.

Somewhere near the center, was all I could deduce. Each door I silently passed stood identical to the previous, until (somewhere in proximity to the hall's mid-point) I stopped to stare at the tiniest brass emblem mounted upon the door I currently faced. Inscribed upon this plaque were, I'm utterly certain, the cuneiformic markings that denoted the following numerals: 1852.

I checked both ways down the hall, was satisfied I was not being surveilled, then stooped to one knee, and to the ornately plated keyhole, I then put my wide-open eye . . .

It troubles me that I cannot in any accuracy convey to you the details I now beheld. It was a spectacular bed-chamber displayed to my clandestine view: sumptuous carpet and wall-coverings, lovely antique furniture and in addition a veiled four-poster bed whose gorgeously carved post and headboard appeared adorned in gold leaf; oil portraits and statuary that were no doubt high-mark collector's items. These facts, however, rendered the chamber *nondescript* when compared to the room's (and I'm not sure I can even summon an adequate term) *sensorial bearing* . . .

There seemed to be a light that was not light but some peculiar cast unlike any I'd observed. This *counter-luminescence (*somehow foggy yet clarity-sharpening) made the room and its contents fairly shimmer as if through mist; and seemed preternaturally magnified via some phantasmal *lens-obscura*, and to that I must not fail to add . . .

Two rod-like objects stood upright at either side of the grand bed. These objects were likely simple wooden dowels (nothing peculiar there) but what covered the top half of each was a mass of some unidentifiable substance that seemed to be partly translucent and rather ill-hued. The only simile I can summon is to say that these poles looked like bunches of wizened white grapes on a stick.

"There you are," issued the unmistakable and faintly accented voice of Madam Aheb. She immediately stepped into view from the rightward side of the key-way, and it was the paste-faced conductor to whom she spoke. The madam's black hair as well as the diaphanous, low-cut gown iridesce'd in the bizarre accentuation of the room's light.

Her voice turned scolding, "And it certainly *took* you long enough to get here. You know how I can't abide to have this awful *stuff* on me for a minute longer that it need be."

I could only see the conductor's back from this voyeuristic vantage point, yet the capped, heavy-jacketed man appeared to bow his head at Miss Aheb's remark of disapproval.

"But of course, I'm aware you and the Thogg were preparing the trolley for the next ingression . . ."

My head turned atilt. *Thogg?* What was *that?* And what did she mean by *ingression?* And what was this 'awful stuff' she'd referred to? What I'd seen thus far assured me there was nothing at all awful about how she appeared.

"I'm ready now," Madam Aheb said and sat eloquently in a spectacular spoke-backed Revolution-era chair.

My view of her was blocked when the conductor stood in front of the madam and, with a linen towel, appeared to be wiping off her arms, shoulders, and graceful legs. "Good, good," she half-moaned. The conductor's hands kept busy in their task but remained a frustrating visual blockage to exactly *what* was being done. Nevertheless, he continued to wipe the exposed skin of his mastress.

What in the name of Pegana is he wiping off? I pondered.

Still blocked by the bulk shape, Miss Aheb stood up from the chair; and it was the movements of the conductor that led me to believe he was now removing the madam's gown.

"Ah, there. That's better. I just so much prefer to be naked . . ."

When the silent conductor stepped away, Miss Aheb stood in full view to my prying eye—

The image forced me to press my hand across my lips; otherwise the horrific image of what I now saw would've surely caused me to scream quite blood-curdlingly . . .

I was looking at a dichotomy of unspeakable magnitude: a collision of *obscene and utter opposites* stripped bare; indeed, the *force majeure* of physical beauty and physical horror. I say, Miss

Aheb now stood naked, and in her nakedness came the accentuation of the sum of all her parts: flawless contours and perfect feminine lines; the sweep of impeccable legs; a sleekness that was robust and healthily slender simultaneously; and high-riding, distendedly nippled breasts that existed without flaw.

The *horror* was in her *complexion.*

Any impeccability of Miss Aheb's physique was howlingly counter-weighed by what I could only conceive of as some ghastly epidermal defect or pitiable disease. Every square inch of her exposed skin was made appalling by a condition far worse than the pallor, say, of the conductor's face but instead by a *skin-tone* that was absolutely revolting. It was not the strange *un-light* that held dominion in the room: of this I was sure. It was a physical fact of the woman's heredity.

Her skin looked like the unpleasant white of a bullfrog's belly marbled by swaths of a mucoid green.

The image nearly overpowered me; I nearly voided my stomach's contents. It occurred to me now that what the servile conductor had been wiping off was no doubt some mode of cosmetic make-up to conceal the madam's true appearance to this evening's guests; what's more (and I don't know how I knew this) I felt all-too-certain that this aberrancy of Miss Aheb's skin was her natural condition!

Between her protuberant yet malignantly toned breasts hung a modest pendant whose elongated stone reminded me of a common stalactite of chalcedony, nearly colorless and rather lackluster. Yet from the thin, two-inch-long stone, after I stared a moment, I took note of the pendant's only *un*common characteristic . . .

It seemed to, however irreducibly, generate some aspect of the room's overall *anti-light.* And as this registered, my eyes slowly roved upward to the most macabre chandelier I've ever beheld. Uneven elongated crystals hung from each setting in the same stalactite fashion (*hundreds* of them, each quite similar to the pendant) inexplicably giving off the light that was not light.

Miss Aheb grinned to her servant in an almost vulturine way. "I simply adore you so much," came a wanton whisper and with it her gracile hand to the conductor's crotch. "Kiss me now . . ."

The conductor's gloved hand came to his chin—

"No, no," the appalling-skinned madam interjected. "Keep the mask on—"

So I was right! I thought. *It was a mask the conductor wore!*

"—I want you *hideous* at first," she continued. "I want you *repulsive!* It makes my juices flow all the more hotly . . ."

I forced my thoughts to still, and merely watched—

—as the conductor's waxen face lowered to Miss Aheb's, and their mouths joined.

Minutes passed; the oral contact roused Miss Aheb noticeably. She stood in a slowly rising craze as the mouth-hole of the conductor's abhorrent mask ranged from her lips and down the slope of her scum-hued throat, then lower to suck into its lurid parchment aperture each gorged nipple.

"Yes, yes," panted the raven-haired madam. "Harder . . . That's just . . . so . . . lovely . . ."

The conductor continued his ministration until a veritable *gloss* of excitement effused from Miss Aheb's vulval groove and shined down the insides of her thighs. Eventually, rapid-breath'd, she pushed her servant's counterfeit mouth away and ordered, "Get the thogg. I'm ready now . . ."

There's that strange word again, I mused. *Thogg . . .*

While the conductor parted, Madam Aheb lay back on the high, plush bed and crudely brought her knees to her face, whereupon her mal-coloured hand began to titillate the furred pubis. Again, I was in paresis from the dichotomy of her unflawed curves made monstrous by the mysterious skin disease.

When the conductor returned he brought with him the equally masked motorman . . .

No words were spoken then as the demented procedure began.

My stomach quivered, for when the bulky motorman displayed his hand, I recalled my impressions when I'd glimpsed it getting off the trolley, dismissing a trick of moonlight as the cause for my initial alarm.

I now saw the *fact* of the matter.

It was no real hand that existed at the end of the motorman's arm but instead a hideous facsimile: a cluster of elongations of boneless, jointless flesh. Just as harrowing, though, was the *hue* of the boneless flesh: the same grub-white spotted by pond-scum green.

First, these fingers, if one could call them that, extended, then wriggled; and then they curled inward to form a parody of a fist which then incredibly swelled in size, then shrank, swelled, then shrank, as if throbbing with some unearthly pulse. Miss Aheb seemed delighted by the demonstration, her splayed legs tensing and buttocks writhing at the sight. Next, her fingers parted the shining lips of her vulva within the nest of hair—a lewd invitation.

Without abatement, the motorman contorted the boneless digits forward and inserted his "hand" into the teeming, pink purse of Miss Aheb's vaginal vault . . .

In and out, then, the monstrous hand delved, begetting a regular slick, wet sound that reminded me of one trudging through mud, the digits obscenely undulating and obviously heightening the pleasure of his (or I should say *its*) mastress. Soon the derrick-like penetrations probed deeper, to the extent that Miss Aheb's reproductive orifice had swallowed the motorman's hand nearly to the point of *mid-forearm* . . .

"Now," the abyssally-skinned woman panted. Her pleasures mounted to tighten every muscle and tendon in her body.

It was to the stoic conductor that the order was directed, for first he removed his gloves, then woolen regulation-blue jacket, then the white shirt beneath . . .

Expression *gaping,* I now beheld the length of this evil ruse: when the conductor's clothes were tossed aside, his nudity revealed him to be no "he" at all, but a woman, and one with a physique nearly as comely as Madam Aheb's.

My shock racked me at my peeper's post.

But the conductor (or I should say now the conduc*tress*) even in her stunning beauty, shared some of the same hideous dichotomy as the madam and this "thogg": that nauseous sickly white skin-tone blended with the mucous-green splotches.

The carnal aberration I bore witness too now was surely a scene forged in hell . . .

Butternut hair fell when the regulation cap was undonned, and then the conductress removed the parchment mask . . .

Simultaneously I felt on the precipice of cardiac failure and a fit of madhouse screaming. How I was able to stave off both, I know not. But this was the *coup de grace* of all I'd visually attested to thus far: the revelation of the conductress's face, which I suspect the perseverant reader has already deduced.

It was my sister *Selina's face* that had been until now secreted beneath the gruesome mask.

What has that hideous BITCH done to my sister! my thoughts railed. Dangling between Selina's ample yet similarly discolored breasts was a pendant like that of Miss Aheb; this I could glimpse as my either brainwashed or subjugated sibling turned for a moment, knelt up on the bed, and then lowered her mouth to her superior's clitoral nub. All the while the motorman's unearthly hand plungered wickedly in and out . . .

"Yes, yes," issued the accented hiss. "Lick it faster, dear, faster." Dung-brown nipples erected to inflamed teepees as the order was complied with. Meanwhile, as if by psychic cue, the dead-faced motorman finally withdrew the marauding forearm while the madam's bare foot caressed the thing's trousered crotch. A lump hardened there and with the attendant stimulation, this less-than-human being lowered said trousers—

I nearly fell into a swoon!

—to reveal genitals as monstrous as its facsimile for a hand.

Indeed, less-than-human was no exaggeration; I could only thank Selina and Erwin's God that it retained the parchment mask, for by now I could not, would not contemplate what its true face must be.

"What a beautiful cock," the madam profaned, eyes enkindled by the throbbing sight.

From the wax-white and utterly hairless groinal region, an identically waxen *prong* of queer white flesh stuck out. I estimated the erect pudenda's length at roughly eight inches, with perhaps two inches' girth at the base. It seemed to lack the sheathing skin as one would typically expect, and tapered queerly to a fleshy point rather than sporting an also-expected dome of glans; I could only think absurdly of a paste-white carrot. Blue traceries of veins ghosted beneath its dread whiteness as it throbbed; likewise, it shined as if effusing its own preludial lubrication. The only aspect that made this vision more hideous was the curious absence of scrotum and, hence, testes.

Selina's next instruction didn't have to be voiced; she held back her madam's legs to more effectively part the groove of the shapely buttocks.

"Now, now," Miss Aheb seethed—

—and it was into her nethermost aperture that the motorman—this *thogg*—inserted the macabre phallus and began to pelvically thrust; all the while, Selina re-tended her superior's swollen clitoral *metus.* The sought-after effect took little time; soon Miss Aheb's hideously skinned yet voluptuously curved body began to buck madly on the bed as the obvious crisis of her climax was at hand. She shrieked, then whinnied as the spasms of release began to pulse—a sound barely human, while in concurrence the motorman's frame stiffened, then began to quiver.

"I can feel it!" Miss Aheb lewdly rejoiced. "Pouring into me! *Filling* me!"

The denouement wound down; then, the motorman withdrew its carrot-like "cock" from the woman's bowel. My sister turned away, appalled.

"That was lovely, dear," Miss Aheb commended. She lay slit-eyed and grinning, the quaking orgasms leaving her limp on the plush bed. "But now that I've had my moment . . . You know what to do . . ."

The thogg stepped away, stuffing his sullied organ back into his trousers; yet my sister, in motions that were clearly gruelling, came round to kneel at the edge of the bed between the madam's upthrust thighs.

"I just can't abide the idea of the thogg's jism being in me for long," Miss Aheb remarked as Selina pressed her lips to the plumbed sphincter and began to suck.

"There, good, good, dear. Suck it all out . . ."

Numbed to stupefaction, all I could do was watch as poor Selina engaged in the revolting process of evacuating Miss Aheb's rectal vault of the thogg's semen. When her face came away from the cleft, she wobbled on her knees.

"Swallow now, dear," the madam dictated, "and then you'd both best be on your way."

Selina stared in the chandelier's sinister *unlight,* lips pursed as her mouth obviously remained full of the creature's spermatic void. She steeled herself, went tense, then audibly swallowed.

I watched then as my sister rose to listlessly redress herself and re-don the grim parchment mask.

Miss Aheb indicated the strange poles standing to either side of the bed. "The carriers are full as you can see. Take them now—the back stairs as usual, and be on your way through the ingression brink."

At this incomprehensible command, Selina lifted up one of the poles while the motorman hoisted up the other. These poles or rods or whatever they were continued to mystify me. What exactly was the mass of shriveled, semi-lucent things adhered to them? Again, I thought of wizened grapes . . .

Miss Aheb stood up, her nude body stunning in its curvatures yet appalling in its discolor. "Go in glory," she oddly bid my sister, "and sing praise to our benefactors."

Here was the only occasion for a vocal utterance on Selina's part. "Yes, Madam Aheb."

"And have the trolley back by bell-time. Soon our very generous guests will have had their fill of the evening's delights." She grinned wickedly in the shimmering light that was not light. "As we so have our fill of *them* . . ."

Selina and the motorman departed through an adjoining door and disappeared. I was able to detect the sound of descending footfalls . . .

They're going down a set of ancillary stairs, I realized, *to the trolley.*

My own footfalls took me in haste, down the sweeping main stairs to the atrium; I realized the import of moving faster than my sister and the cumbersome motorman, and was confident of this goal's achievability. From each stair-hall I detected the sounds of sexual traffic (moans, murmurs, squeals of lascivious release) and was relieved to find the atrium devoid of prostitutes and male suitors alike. At once I passed through the large outer door to the decrepit courtyard, and in the moon's bedimmed light, I boarded the vacant trolley and piloted myself to the rearmost seats of the second car, to hide myself. Before I'd stowed my person behind the wood-slat seat, however, I paused to take further note of that great archway of lichen-stained blocks embrasuring the mammoth door of rusted iron beams studded with rivets. Again I was perplexed by the almost mirage-like image: a sickly colored *mist* that seemed impossibly oily, sifting beneath the great door's gap; and with it, evidence of some weird half-light that I was now able to correspond to the indefinable shimmer of Miss Aheb's bed-chamber.

What could possibly be behind the door that would possess such strange traits? This was New York City, for goodness sake . . .

I ducked back down, as the footsteps I knew would come had arrived. I heard my sister and her monstrous companion clatter aboard the trolley. Exposing myself to an obvious risk, I dared to steal a split-second peek above the seat-back's edge . . .

Selina and the motorman—that *thing*—had planted the pair of mass-cloaked rods in mounts of some sort or other, where they now stood upright as they had upstairs. Selina tended to some flicking of switches on a control board, but it was the motorman who dismounted and plodded toward the massive arched door.

A loud metallic *clang!* reverberated as a bolt was thrown, then came the keening grind of old hinges as the thing secreted beneath the garb of a transit motorman pulled open the doors.

With half an eye over the seat-back, I stared in utter befuddlement . . .

More stone blocks filled the archway, rendering passage impossible! *What on earth?* I thought. Yet the negating blocks were not of normal stone, as were those of the arch and the courtyard's walls . . .

They were of the same cryptic material that comprised the stalactitical crystals of Miss Aheb's chandelier, and her and Selina's pendants!

The trolley jerked; metal abraded as the vehicle's wheels squealed over the ancient rails, and it was then . . .

Impossible!

Trolley No. 1852 rumbled forward toward the *solid wall* within the arch and—

Ineptly, I covered my head with my arms, awaiting what . . . I could never estimate.

The trolley, without so much as a hitch, *passed through* the wall of outerworldly blocks.

There came a noisome *sucking* sound, then one of soft grinding; I myself felt as though I were being pulled through a range of sand, yet no physical substance was observed; barely visible mist, however, *was* observed, akin to the seeming mist I'd thought I noticed in the madam's chamber. I received the notion that the mist (warm and somehow oily) existed in some direct or indirect relativity to that inexplicable counter-luminescence, for that same trait now—that light which was *not* light—held dominion over the queer space in which the trolley now ranged.

And a queer space it was, indeed.

I sensed *barrenness* even before I opened my eyes, and felt inordinate pressure as well as a peculiar absence of air temperature; it was neither hot nor cold, just simply *nothing.* I thought of vacuities and voids, of inhuman realms and lost worlds. It was then that I actually looked out of the trolley-car's vestibule . . .

Should this manuscript ever be found, I suspect that by this point, the reader will have no choice but to dismiss me as one fit for some refuge for the deranged. Translating what I then witnessed into communicable lexicon would overbound the skill of even the most preeminent writer. Sufficient words, you see, simply do not exist. I will endeavor, though, toward a feeble attempt . . .

I saw a sky hazy with the anti-light, whose source could not be perceived as there was no object of provenance, such as a sun or a moon. Yet beyond the spectral shimmer, the nature of this phenomenon I can only think of as a sky existed in layers, or *stratum,* the darkest being the most elevated, the lightest being in the closest proximal relation to the land, if indeed it could be called as such. Yet each strata bore colours defying category; instead, they seemed gradient shades of tone, bereft of what we're taught to be primary and/or secondary colouring which, when amalgamated, result in the visual character of what our eyes perceive. Forgive my convolutedness, and I apologize for any ensuant frustration. Alas, this is the only description my anaemic grey-matter can generate.

Even more spectral, though, than this "sky" was the terrain itself over which the clattering trolley now traversed. The physical realm I now beheld (what I mean is the solid ground) existed not as earth nor desert, not as hillock nor woodland. It was merely flat, barren *space,* flat to exactitude and extending as far as the eye could register retinal images. I knew then that I must be on another planet, or (recalling the forbidden mythologies of the ancient Ahebites) within some other dimensional plane that existed in contestation with the three aspects of dimensionality we are comfortable with; for the Ahebites, led by the dread witch-priestess Isimah el-Aheb, were worshipers and human physical agents for the drab, featureless beings known as the Pyramidiles who did indeed inhabit a realm that was not planetary and thereby could only be para-dimensional.

This, I knew, was but grim fable; or at least I'd always *thought* it to be . . .

How, though, could I deny it *now?*

More surveillance was necessary for me to make a proper assessment of this *phantasmata* I was now sitting in the middle of. I required a forward view, which would no doubt expose me to the greatest risk yet. Nevertheless, I took my chance, realising no other subsidiary manoeuvre.

I stood upright at the back of the trolley.

What faced me were the backs of my sister and the aberrant motorman; nothing could be more imperative, I knew, than to prevent them from seeing me. Yet *I* was the one who needed to see. And *see* I did . . .

To my unabating horror.

Past the shoulders of Selina and the *thogg* there stretched a vista so strange, so unutterably alien, that the very glimpsing of it fleeced the breath from my lungs and instigated a slugging of my heart. It was a horizon of sorts, extending to sheer endlessness, a screaming, demented infinity that transcended all manner of measure. Sounds like wicked wind blended with some *human* aspect seemed to shriek from all directions; and dust (though dust that glittered) flitted through the ultra-terrestrial haze, filtering a purview of impossibility. The only apparent "natural" objects in view were the two track-rails extending in perfect linearity for incalculable miles ahead. *Who could possibly have lain them?* I wondered in fascinated terror. *And just how long do they extend?*

These and myriad more questions overflowed in my struggling and shock-wearied mind. This land and sky of undefected planes, I knew, could not exist via any known laws of nature or relativity, nor could the trolley's very passage—a vehicle with no perceptible mode of power. But my unblinking eyes bloomed then, when the flat, vacuous void ahead at last relinquished some of its unfathomable homogeneousness, the blistering panorama's monotony finally breaking to reveal the tiniest eruptions of some facet of *feature.*

Pyramids! I realised through a headache-inducing squint.

Yes, miles or hundreds of miles distant, their ranks rose as the trolley approached: a morass of pyramid-shaped objects whose angles all existed in perfect uniformity. Some spired higher than others, but beyond that, they were all of the same, and I knew now what they could only be . . .

The Pyramidiles.

That hideous race of faceless, immobile *anti-beings* so decadently and blood-thirstily revered by the Ahebites of pre-dynastic Egypt.

It's true! It's all true! my palpitating thoughts screamed.

The myth of the Pyramidiles was no myth; so then neither could be their principal servitor on earth, the witch-priestess Isimah el-Aheb, now known as Madam Aheb of the 1852 Club . . .

And it was into the midst of these appalling parasites of undying turmoil that the trolley ventured. God only knew what would happen once we arrived.

Whether it was hours which lapsed, or days, the prospect was beyond my mental potency to estimate. Neither Selina nor the noxious motorman moved from their forward posts, but eventually, the range of minuscule pyramidic eruptions grew larger as more distance was gained; then, hours or days later . . . they *loomed,* and in their looming I stood utterly paralyzed. The smallest of them stood hundreds of feet high, yet the tallest easily spired thousands of feet into the obscure, unilinear stratum above; each Pyramid was indeed a colossus; and being cognizant that each of these things were alive made the observation all the more horrific. That incessant living wind-like screaming rose in pitch as the trolley clattered directly into the thick of the things. I could see them and their mammoth flesh-walls; could *see* the most horrific trait of all: whatever it was that covered their living pyramidal bodies (presumably some foreign laminae that served as skin) was of a wet, sickly white, like that of a bullfrog's belly, tessellated with an even more sickly green.

Just like the skin of Miss Aheb and Selina . . .

It was an uncontemplatable labyrinth that existed between the bases of these horrid, titan creatures; and through that labyrinth the trolley now wended. I thought of a lone skiff coursing betwixt glaciers, or the most meager train locomoting between the most enormous mountains. The Pyramidiles' "skin" made me physically ill to behold, yet now, given their size when compared to our proximity, it was all I could see to either side. The slimy dermis shivered as we passed, showing revolting dilating pores that shuddered as if via some mode of respiration. Great hoselike lines swerved in every direction, pulsing–and I knew that these could only be the things' veins. But in veins flowed *blood,* circulated by *hearts,* and it was the nature of such that I would've preferred to kill myself than to speculate or, worse, bear witness to. Just as frightening queries, however, did race mad through my mind; for one: How much space did these appalling hulks of flesh occupy? Dozens of square miles? Thousands? *More?*

The trolley stopped.

I ducked to re-conceal myself behind the seat just as my horribly masked sister turned. Two sets of footsteps on metal told me that she and the motorman had debarked . . .

Now was my chance, risky as it may have been, to make a closer examination of the two poles covered with the inexplicable masses, but I knew I must be very careful and very quick.

A peek over the side showed me Selina and her grim attendant walking down a queer lane formed between two of the monstrous pyramids of flesh. On hands and knees, then, I traversed the entirety of the rear car's aisle, hopped across the coupling, and continued as such to the trolley's forward area, and slid into the footwell of a seat nearest the debarkation steps. Small oval holes had been cut out at the bottom of the vehicle's sideboards (likely for drainage during rain) so with my cheek to the floor I again looked out. There was no sign of my sister or the motorman . . .

Next, my hands and knees took me to the simple mounts into which the bizarre dowels had been erected.

What in the name of . . .

This close I was easily able to discern the strange substance which composed the "wizened masses" that the poles were designed to carry. Easy to discern, quite, but easy to cogitate?

By no means.

These masses that could be likened to bunches of shriveled grapes were actually multiple hundreds of unrolled prophylactic sheaths. Each had been fixed to dozens of outward pointing metal rods spouting from the dowel; and onto each more than several of the barrier sheaths had been fixed via tiny clips. Each dangled limply, weighted at its end by the portion of human sperm that had been jettisoned into it. *Rows and rows of soiled condoms, two veritable TREES of them,* came my outrageous yet clearly incontestable observation. It was to these outlandish "trees" that the club's harlots had been clipping the spent, vulcanised barriers all along; and no doubt for a considerable time—many days, I would reckon, or more than likely many weeks . . .

I ducked back, to hide myself again several seats rearward, not knowing what to do or what even to think. Moments later, the footsteps re-boarded, and a peek around the side showed my masked sister lifting one of the dowels from its mount, and the grub-handed motorman lifting the other. Again, then, they debarked, carrying with them the sperm-laden dowels . . .

When I peered through the current drainage port, I gasped; for now, standing before the trolley were a dozen hideous, naked *creatures* beyond the stuff of nightmare. Their hands and openly displayed penises existed identically to that which I'd seen of the motorman during his service to Miss Aheb. However, unlike said motorman, these wore nothing, and had no parchment masks—which was surely the worst part, for their faces . . . Their faces . . .

The pallid things sported faces that were but drooping cones of the alien flesh; each cone tapering to single scarlet-tipped tentacle. I shuddered where I lay. The things (*thoggs,* I could only presume, the same devilish, outerworldly species as the motorman) stood bereft of eyes, nostrils, ears, and mouths. What is more, though they stood upright on two mucilaginous legs, there seemed no evidence of any joints where elbows, knees, and ankles should be. Boneless, in other words, utterly lacking in ossification. Their penises dangled obscenely at the joists of their legs. And, save for their bellies and genital regions which were an exclusive pasty-white, the rest of their skin shimmered in identical hue to that of Miss Aheb and Selina: that awful white covered by greenish swirls and splotches . . .

Two of the horrendous beasts took the poles and disappeared with them, while the others appeared to be in some sort of non-verbal concert with Selina, though how this could be, I could scarcely ideate. *What are they doing?* my thoughts ground like old hinges, for upon sensing some instruction from the most paramount thogg, my sister's head drooped as if disheartened.

Then she began to disrobe.

I could only presume that these naked monstrosities served as common laborers (proles) to tend to various duties that the mammoth Pyramidiles required—such as the aforementioned: the collection and redeposition of human reproductive discharge. Evidently, however, their toil was on occasion rewarded; as it was clear that my poor sister had been ordered to sexually avail herself to these ghastly things, as some mode of recreational release . . .

Once stripped naked and unmasked, my sister turned, posing her beautifully formed yet hideously discolored body for the sensorial pleasure of these things. It was as though even without eyes, they could somehow *see* her physique's enticing attributes, the positive reaction of which was more than apparent. The thoggs' penises, tapered like waxen carrots, erected with promptitude; while the overall image remained somehow more revolting by their absence of scrotums and sequent testicles.

Selina lowered herself to the strange polychromatic soil and parted her legs . . .

The first of the nauseating things diminished no time in mounting her and burying its inhuman pudenda into her sex. The pallid rump rapidly cycled up and down (all quite perfunctorily) until its climax was achieved and the thing was slaked. Then the next one mounted her, and the next, and the next after that. As each of the creatures neared the point of orgasmic crisis, the suckerless tentacle dangling from its face turned a deeper scarlet, as if to denote excitement. Then more came, and more . . .

Though Selina had not been physically forced to submit to the abhorrent beasts, this sufficed for rape *en masse* nonetheless. I cried as morbidity forced me to watch further. My first impulse, of course, had been to take the thoggs by surprise and give fight, but this I knew was useless as it was futile. Surely I'd be overpowered and killed with relative simplicity and, hence, never be able to rescue Selina from this wretched supernatural plight. What dejected me all the more was the angle at which Selina had arranged herself for the monstrous submission: her parted thighs and splayed buttocks directed precisely toward the port from which I observed, which only afforded me a depressingly accurate view of the actual coitus. I was forced to watch as each unearthly phallus divided my sister's sexual folium and slid all of its tumescent length into her. It was from these monstrous loins that their seed was thereby transferred into the loins of my poor sister; and it was quite an abundant transfer, indeed, for upon satisfaction the current creature withdrew to make way for the next, but not before a *flood* of their sexual fluids issued out like so much effluence, leaving a great and widening tarn of the stuff between Selina's pried-wide legs. It was that strange *anti*-light, I knew, that lent blade-sharp clarity and preternatural magnification to this bitter effusion; for even as my distance from the scene exceeded twenty feet, I saw details as though they were just inches away, which served to only heighten my disconsolation; and even more regrettably, this visual enhancement detailed to me the very *inhumanness* of the thoggs' discharge. I could only surmise that even in the thoggs' lack of visible testes, they were obviously possessed of *ample* seminal vesicles and prostates of the stoutest kind, and as for the semen itself?

It was like no man's semen at all, but thicker, more opaque, akin to semi-curdled buttermilk but laced with threads of resolute black, like squid ink.

My outrage began to roil from within: these abyssal things were utilising the cavity of my poor sister's womanhood as a *receptacle* of brute lust, and there was nothing I could do about it. I was left with no recourse but to cringe and silently sob.

It was the ninth or tenth thogg who forewent intercourse and opted instead to audaciously straddle Selina about her belly. Into her mammarian valley its waxen penis was lain; whereupon it *cocooned* said penis by pressing both breasts inward, forming a seat for false-coital purchase. The splotched buttocks, then, rocked back and forth, drawing the dread phallus in and out of the compressed vale, and when the sought-after moment arrived—

Selina groaned.

—my sister grimly inclined her head in time to allow repeated spurts of the monster's seed to be jettisoned into her opened mouth via the thogg's aboriginal replication of the sin of Onan: masturbation. The alarming voluminousness of its seminal product did, upon completion of the unnatural act, in all truth fill my sister's oral cavity right up to the brim of her lips. Even without a face the thogg glared down as if in some scolding expectancy, and that is when my most unfortunate sibling swallowed the entire mouthful. The sight had a nearly emetic effect on my own stomach, knowing that all that evil sperm had been swallowed into hers; yet I wished I could swoon or even die when I next watched *two more* thoggs fill Selina's mouth similarly, producing, if anything, *more* ejaculant than the previous contributor.

All of it was swallowed.

A final creature finished the foray by copulating with and spending itself into Selina's bowel.

My GOD, my thoughts quaked when it was over.

Some sensibilities returned when I knew that this heinous victimisation was (for now, at least) at a terminus. But one point had eloped from my mind whilst witnessing the gruesome proceeding:

The motorman, I realised.

He had not joined in the festivities with his diabolic brethren, unless he'd somehow gotten shed of the mask and regulation uniform without my seeing. *Perhaps he went unseen to tend to some encumbrance or other for the Pyramidiles,* I considered, *Or perhaps—*

From where I crouched in hiding, I felt a tap upon my shoulder; and in horrific slowness, I turned my head and looked up . . .

The motorman loomed above me, still clothed but unmasked now, and somehow glowering, however facelessly. The tentacle sprouting from the drooping splotch-fleshed cone where its face *should've* been, jiggled hideously, the tip reddened as if dipped in blood.

God save me, I prayed for the first time in my life.

The motorman shot its boneless hands downward, latched onto my shoulders, and dragged me up; and as if I weighed no more than a grasp of straw, I was flung over the vestibule to land with a shuddering thud upon the dead, lackluster soil of this deranged place. At once I was surrounded by the troop of naked, flaccid-penised thoggs.

Selina raised herself to elbows, the pain of this surprise plain on her face. "Oh, Morgan, you shouldn't have done this. Coming to the club was bad enough but now? Stowing away on the trolley? You've no idea what peril you've put yourself in . . ."

Winded, I staggered to my feet. "I've been searching for you for years, Selina," I nearly wept. "And now that I've found you, I know I must do everything in my power to rescue you from this, this *evil.*"

"There can be no rescuing, Morgan—it's impossible. Miss Aheb will never let me go, and these thoggs are undefeatable. This is my plight now, and it will never change unless Miss Aheb grows weary of me."

"Weary? Selina, I don't understand."

"When it started out, I was just one of the working girls at the club. Free food and shelter, in *this* economy? We were starving on the street, Morgan. The club provided us with an arrangement none of us could refuse," she explained. "But Miss Aheb soon took a *personal* fancy to me, and I would no longer service the johns, only her, plus other duties . . . like *this.*"

What an atrocious subjugation, I thought but even as a hundred questions occurred to me, I was prevented from giving voice to a single one, for the most brutish of the naked thoggs shoved me roughly and pointed with a jointless finger down to where my sister lay.

"The thoggs are ultimately vicious," Selina told me with a tear in her eye, "and ultimately perverse."

The thing shoved me again but for a reason that alluded me.

"It wants you . . . to fuck me, Morgan," came my sister's groaning voice. "They want to watch."

I stood aghast. "I could never in a million y—"

"Morgan, sick as it is, you *must.*"

"But that's incest!" I outraged. "The most irredeemable of nature's aberrations!"

She sobbed openly now. "If you don't . . . they'll kill you. But you can be guaranteed that it will be a very slow death. The thoggs are bred for torture, Morgan. They *exist* to inflict pain, and they're very good at it."

I turned to the most salient of them. "Then so be it! You'll not coerce me to defile my sister, you pestiferous, para-dimensional degenerate! Go ahead and kill me!"

Two of the things grabbed my arms, but it was not toward me that the commandant embarked. It was toward Selina.

It fell on her at once, and when she screamed it was into her opened mouth that the ghastly beast inserted its boneless hand. Meanwhile one of the others did the same to her sex, until they were both *reaching into her* from either direction. I sensed all too clearly that they intended to eviscerate Selina, trans-orally and trans-vaginally.

"Stop!" I bellowed so loud I feared my eyes would leap from their sockets. "I consent to your demand!"

Had the things been able to grin, I'm certain they'd have been doing so now. They removed their offending hands from Selina's body, while some psychic command urged her to position herself on hands and knees. Now it was *I* who sobbed openly; to my own knees I then fell, and unfastened my trousers.

The pallid monsters clustered closer around, their eyeless faces intent on the scenario. I concentrated on the plushness of Selina's rump while forcing myself not to perceive the grotesque skin-tone. My member, however, hung limp, useless.

I croaked. "Selina, I can't possibly grow sufficiently aroused under *these* circumstances! You're my *sister!*"

"You have to try," she panted, and shot a pleading glance over her shoulder. "They'll kill us both . . ."

Humiliated, I stroked my flaccid flesh, all to no effect. More inhibiting was the notion that I was being spectated by not only the revolting thoggs but by the immense Pyramidiles who towered all about. All the while, my member remained very grimly *un*erect; and while Ammi and her slatternly sorority back at the club had marveled over its ostensibly greater-than-average size when inflamed, this situation's horror left it anything but. I stroked on in futility, while I knew that however voicelessly, the thoggs were laughing at its pitiable size.

"Let me help," my sister whispered, and up betwixt her own legs came her hand, to gently manipulate my penis. *I MUST perform to their satisfaction,* I focused on the thought and its severity, *otherwise both of our lives could end in this wretched place . . .*

"Just relax, relax," she whispered further, fingers first tending my slack testicles, then the even more slack shaft, and then—

Perhaps the decadent French writers were correct in their esoteric allusions to a link between death and sexuality (their *La Petite Morte*) for the more I focused on the possibility that impotence would result in our destruction . . .

My member *swelled.*

If anything, the sudden erection sprouted even longer than before—longer than *ever*—until it thumped, bobbing up and down. I knew that the thoggs had been, in their own non-verbal manner, laughing at me before, but—

They're not laughing now, I thought, assured. They could all detect that the dimensions of *my* genital shaft easily exceeded that of even the largest of them. When Selina's hand measured its entire length, she gasped, "Good *gracious,* Morgan. I had no idea you were so . . ."

She needn't finish; instead it may have even been with some secret eagerness that her deft fingers brought my purpled glans to her folds.

"Now!" she panted.

I nudged it in, then grasped her hips and commenced to stroking. The familiar wet slapping resounded as I increased tempo, sliding my erection (each and every of its proven twelve inches) all the way in and all the way out. Simultaneously, my left hand slipped round and under, to gently agitate her surprisingly excited clitoris, and with that,

Selina began to moan with vigor. I stepped up my pelvic rhythm then, pursuing a crescendo; whereupon my sister quite waveringly squealed. Her back arched like that of a cat; every tendon in her body tensing; and then her climax spasmed and broke most obviously. She writhed and bucked, even shrieked to the capacity of her lungs, to the extent that the blissful vociferation echoed within the vast valleys between the mammoth Pyramidiles. I cursed myself for acknowledging my own incestuous pleasure, for as her orgasm drew on quite lengthily, Selina's interior vagina constricted to an unfathomable tautness which brought me past the margin of my own return. This next seminal ration *gusted* from my loins in innumerous spurts, and with the release I experienced my own ecstatic culmination, the potency of which I would've never believed possible . . .

When both of our spasms abated, Selina collapsed. "For goodness *sake,* Morgan. Never in my life have I had such a wonderful f—"

"You needn't say it, Selina," I severed her profanity. "As you've directed, we had no choice but to sully ourselves for the whims of these things," but when I looked around I sensed disappointment about the mien of the thoggs, or rather even displeasure. My forced performance for their mere sport seemed to have left them in agitation rather than satisfaction.

Selina sensed it too, obviously attuned to them either by indoctrination or some totemic function of her queer pendant. She even giggled. "They're *jealous,* Morgan."

I refastened my trousers. "Jealous?" I questioned but suddenly the notion made sense. Not only was I possessed of more substantial genitals (the utmost symbol of masculinity) but I had also demonstrated a further degree of sexual superiority over them: my efforts alone had brought Selina to a devastating climax, whereas theirs had not.

"Will they let us go, now that we've done as they ordered?"

Selina knelt as she faced me; her shoulders slumped. "Not . . . just . . . yet . . ."

It was the clothed motorman who approached, then slapped me across the head.

"What?" I blathered. "What is this?"

"They're furious that you out-performed them, Morgan," came my sister's disconsolate reply. "They won't let us go back until you've sufficiently debased yourself. It's their way of getting back at you, for proving that you're more masculine than all of them."

I couldn't imagine what she might be implying, but then imagination was hardly necessary a moment later when the motorman lowered his trousers and extracted the harrowing genitals.

"You have to take him in your mouth," came Selina's regretful words.

"In the name of all things decent and pure!" I caterwauled.

"And you'll have to swallow it all. Only then will they be satisfied . . . That way, they get their last laugh, in spite of your manly prowess . . . by turning you into their bitch, so to speak."

Despair couldn't have lengthened my face further. Since the motorman's release with Miss Aheb, enough time had passed to permit full sexual revivification; the thing was ready again, in other words, and to that state of readiness I could all-too-awfully attest. The grotesque organ had already become engorged by the thing's mere thought of what impended.

"Just do it, Morgan," my sister pleaded. "You don't want to *know* how many times I've had to . . ."

To this end I resigned myself; I'd be doing it not only to spare my own life but Selina's as well. So I steeled myself with every mental fortitude . . . took the appalling thing into my mouth.

Having had no experience in such things, however, I hadn't a clue as to what I was doing. I harnessed initiative only via the deduction that I must do my best to *imagine* the proper technique . . .

In only seconds that dreadful "carrot" hardened to full size in my quivering mouth.

Inept as I was sure my oral subventions were, the motorman

seemed overly pleased by the effort. Each time I drew my lips rearward, along the organ's tapering form, I increased the suction, which caused the beast's hips to fidget.

"Faster now," Selina instructed. "And . . . get ready . . ."

I forced the implication from conscious thought, proceeding as instructed. Then . . .

The motorman's "jism" *poured* into my mouth.

The effect was worse than any conjecture. My face seemed to turn to stone after my first gulp. To assign simile to the *taste* of the evil slew defied possibility. Gout after gout, it issued, each mouth-filling allotment seeming thicker than the previous, and more lumpen.

"Keep swallowing, Morgan!" my sister implored. "Don't spit up!"

Easier communicated than achieved. Numbed to my brain, I forced myself to mechanically pause, then swallow, pause, then swallow. The stuff was hot, and I could swear I actually felt spermatozoic constituents *moving around on my tongue* each time my oral cavity was re-filled. I could only imagine that the forced consumption of carrion or even excreta would be more agreeable than this . . .

I reeled on my knees after the abatement of the motorman's final spurt, that last deposit being thick as gelatin. My stomach threatened to heave and properly eject the violation, but I gathered all my forbearance, fisted my hands, and, shuddering, swallowed the whole gelatinous mass.

"You did it!" Selina congratulated.

When the hideous lump at last sunk to the pit of my squirming gut, I collapsed posthaste into a dead faint.

Two

Some inestimable time later, my senses seemed to rise, akin to putrefactive gases voiding from a lime-pit. It was upon the pristine floor of Miss Aheb's lavish yet eldritchly lit bed-chamber that my consciousness re-found me; in fact, my first sight was that of the corrupt chandelier suspended overhead, shimmering in its queer anti-light.

Of the dimension-transcending trolley-ride back, I remembered nary a detail. I was alone, however, and as I roused myself, I checked my pocket-watch to see, to my dismay, that the time was but four-thirteen in the morn . . .

Only *one minute* later than when I'd checked so long ago!

The watch continued to tick, though, the second-hand revolving . . .

Just like Erwin mentioned. This place, and that horrendous domain I've just returned from, must exist in some daedalic contravention of time . . .

A strange tapping cut into my ruminations, tapping which I recognized eventually as footsteps. It was my sister, maskless but dressed once more in her conductor's garb, who crossed the mosaic flooring. The chamber's bizarre acoustics lent to her voice an uncanny echo. "Oh, Morgan, I'm so sorry about what they made you do."

"It was of my own free volition that I came here in the first place, and of my own free volition that I smuggled myself aboard Trolley 1852," I recited. "All in the interest in finding you."

"You're such a gallant man, Morgan. I can only imagine your disgust with me."

"Disgust?" I asked, irked. "You're my only sibling, and I love you with my whole heart. Please know that."

"But to learn that your only sibling could stoop so low as to submit to prostitution . . ."

"My dearest sister, what you must also know is that I fully understand the travails that force women to resort to such alternatives. In these times of economic cataclysm, women even more than men suffer from the throes of subjugation." Groggily, I sat up. "This, believe me, I comprehend, and I love you no less."

Selina seemed relieved to hear this, relieved enough even to sob. But what I simply could *not* reckon was the hideousness of her maligned complexion, the once-beauteous countenance made appalling by the swirls of phlegmatic-green mixed with fish-belly white. "I had no choice but to consign myself to the life of a common street-whore but even then I was homeless and barely able to eat . . ."

"I *understand* that," I reiterated. "But . . . what I *don't* understand is . . ."

"The change," she finished for me, and touched her face with loath. "Eventually some girls corralled me into the club, but as I briefly explained earlier, I did not service johns for long after my arrival. It turned out, Miss Aheb fell in love with me, so . . . she *changed* me . . ."

"Your skin," I knew. "She effected a metamorphosis, to make your skin like hers"—I gulped—"and like the skin of Pyramidiles and the thoggs."

"With this, yes," she explicated, fingering the pendant. "The change allows me to live forever, but this is what I'll have to do . . . *forever.* She wants me all to herself; and when I'm not servicing her, I conduct the trolley and, every week or so, see to the transport of our . . . collection across the ingression threshold."

Collection, I thought numbly. *The constant collection of human semen to be used for God knows what by the Pyramidiles . . .*

"The legend is true," I droned. "The club's matron, Miss Aheb, and the witch-priestess Isimah el-Aheb of thousands of years bygone are one in the same!"

Did the chandelier's counter-light suddenly climb in intensity? It was Miss Aheb herself who next strode into the chamber, adorned in the diaphanous black gown which highlighted her preeminent physique. Yet the sleek arms and legs, the plunging decolletage, and her face remained abhorrent by her skin's similarity to that of the mountainous Pyramidiles. I knew now that the leviathanic monsters had, through some occult mode, shared their hideous skin with Miss Aheb and Selina. What other traits beyond appearance might this dermal metamorphosis have instigated?

"Why, immortality, Mr. Phillips," the lithe madam answered via some manner of psychic surveillance. Her coy smile beamed down on me as her accent buoyed her words. "You know much of what very few know at all."

"The legend of the Pyramidiles and their utmost servitor is obscure to be sure," I asserted, "but some trace of their history has remained. Cuneiform cylinders analogous to the cylinder in your own possession, for instance. It is a legend that *pre-dates* legendry . . ."

"And therefore?"

My words abraded like stones grinding. "The *oldest* legend in human history."

"Very good," she congratulated and sashayed about Selina. Her grotesque-colored hand caressed my sister's bosom as she did so; whereupon, she proceeded to a great armchair nestled in the room's corner: a *throne* for all intents, composed of adhered jewel-like crystals of the same composition as the pendants. It was here that she sat, elevated and grinning cunningly, as some sluttish, monstrous version of Cleopatra, some iniquitous *queen* of the Halls of Eblis. "And now? Whatever shall we do with you?"

"Answer my questions," I dared. "What harm can there be in that, given that my chances of surviving the night are in all likelihood non-existent."

Her expression turned wanton as she considered my request; likewise, her hands lifted her plenteous breasts out of the accouchement of her gown, where she then titillated herself before me. "Your desire to know is like the lust of a beast in rut, Mr. Phillips. Do you believe that you will be better fortified by such knowledge when I have your life snuffed out?"

"I quite indubitably do."

Her fingertips twirled the papillae of each distended nipple, generating a sensation which caused her to seethe. "Very well . . ."

"In exactitude just what *are* these mountain-sized creatures known as the Pyramidiles?"

Some psychic directive compelled Selina to approach the throne and, with immediacy, bring her lips to Miss Aheb's bosom. "They are so much more than *creatures,* Mr. Phillips, and even so much more than *gods.* I'm surprised a man of your erudite distinction has failed to make that deduction. They are not millions of years old, nor even *billions,* but so much older that their existence transcends time as we know it. They are *ageless.*" She paused to concentrate on the pleasures lent to her via my sister's lips. "Creatures? No. They are poly-sentient bio-machines, self-perpetuating organic industries, Mr. Phillips. They create vast technologies via their immeasurable intellect and then *produce* their own laborers to make those technologies transitive."

"The thoggs," I uttered.

"Oh, yes. But the thoggs you've beheld are but one variety of a multitude. The Pyramidiles breed them, you see, specifically for implementation on *this* planet. There are hundreds more incarnations, for hundreds of other worlds, and when I say 'worlds,' I mean not only other planets in this and other solar systems but also planes of alternate existence in other dimensions and other terrestrial realms the likes of which even an advanced mind such as yours could never cogitate."

"So that awful abode of theirs is not a planet of itself?"

"No, nor is it a dimensional firmament, Mr. Phillips. It is an esoteric terrascape of their *own creation,* just as the thoggs and all their multiple variations are the Pyramidiles' very creation as well."

I felt enslimed by the sheer *evil* of the implication. "And through these vast technologies and with these thoggs, you travel from world to world!" I outraged, "from dimension to dimension and from realm to realm, to unleash *horror* upon the populace of those places!"

"Exactly," she cooed and moved Selina's lips from the current, well-tended nipple to the next. "The thoggs you saw were the bipedal hybrid propagated for *this* world."

"An invasion is what you're talking about!" I shouted.

"Quite right. But this invasion, whenever it might come to pass, will not be initiated for the purpose of conquest."

I knew all too well of the legend's most atrocious entails. "It is instead for the blatant molestation and torture of the human race, the psychic horror of which the Pyramidiles *subsist* upon!"

"It is their food, which they derive from countless worlds and innumerable domains—yes. We've just come from one such domain, a quasi-terrestrial sphere that existed in another phase-shift. It had a population of a trillion, Mr. Phillips, and the slow, systematic torture, mutilation, and protracted murder of its pacifistic inhabitants fed the Pyramidiles full to bursting. It was *glorious.*"

And eventually, they'll do the same here, I realised.

Miss Aheb broadened her sluttish smile. "Yes. They will."

The rest, now, remained fairly elementary. "Depositions of human sperm," I croaked. "This is the purpose of your inviting the most virile of men to this 'free' bordello, and hence the ruse. It's no real bordello at all, but a *collection outpost!* You pilfer the semen from all these men, night after night, then deliver it all to the Pyramidiles whose bio-mechanical capabilities isolate the *human* characteristics that are specifically desired and then immix those characteristics with that of their own!"

"Custom-made thoggs, Mr. Phillips," she went on. "Genetic constituents from human semen is amalgamated with certain constituents belonging to the Pyramidiles. The result: creatures of servitude and utility that are ideally suited to earth's environment." The ardour imparted to her sensitive nipples via Selina's mouth was all-too-ostensible; the noxious woman's chest rose and fell more rapidly, her infernal skin beginning to sheen with perspiration. Still, though, she continued to explain as though this revelation of diabolism was of itself libidinally stimulating. "The average human ejaculation contains hundreds of millions of spermatozoa, Mr. Phillips, yet only several hundred are chosen for propagation: the choicest, most motile and highest quality per batch. That is why it's taken several millennia to produce a serviceable number of thoggs. But since time *per say* is of no significance, what does it matter?"

"It matters quite a bit with regard to your actual mass-dispersal of the heinous creatures upon the earth!" I yelled. "When exactly is this 'invasion' of yours to take place?"

"Only when we've manufactured exactly *two billion* thoggs, Mr. Phillips."

My indignation spilled over. "But that's the human population of the world today!"

"Precisely."

"At least give my race a fighting chance!"

"Really now, Mr. Phillips. Fairness is not on our agenda. Only the efficacious slow-destruction of mankind. I know that the Pyramidiles will enjoy a veritable *feast* on the pain and horror generated at the hands of the thoggs."

By this point my infuriation left me utterly stupefied . . .

Miss Aheb urged my sister's mouth from the well-sucked nipple. "That felt delicious, dear." Her svelte hands directed Selina to the foot of the throne. "Do here now, my darling," and then she raised the hem of the gown. "You know how I simply adore your mouth on me."

Selina knelt before the madam's parted thighs, then lowered her face . . .

More, more outrage. "Release her! You've demeaned her enough for tonight!"

The atrocious woman's brow rose on the tainted face. "Oh, but not just her, Mr. Phillips. You too, yes?"

"Indeed," I growled.

"Tell me. How did the motorman's jism taste? Was it delectable? Ambrosial? Hmm? I've a mind to send you back there, where you'll be forced to suckle their cocks for time immemorial." She chuckled rather fatly, closing her eyes against the pleasures now being administered. "I can arrange it so that the wares of their lusty loins will be all you ever eat—*ever*—for a million years."

"Give my sister her freedom, and I will consent to that!" I spat.

"Consent? Oh, Mr. Phillips. Your chivalry is quite laughable. I hardly require your *consent* to do with you as my fancies direct." She pressed the back of my sister's head, to affect keener purchase, then looked at me again and laughed.

Being forced to watch this further exploitation insinuated a feeling of utter uselessness on my part. Whatever excess of intellect I may have been possessed of seemed just as useless, for my faculties delivered nothing in so much as a plan of action. Primordially, at least, I might try to give direct fight to Miss Aheb, but being apprised of her powers—for instance, of psychic thought-decryption—I could only imagine that far greater proclivities were at her disposal; while I also suspected that the motorman must be lurking about in some reasonable proximity. I tried to dim the tenor of my conscious thoughts, therefore (to keep them out of her telepathic grasp) and pray that some *sub*conscious resolution might spring to mind.

Her hips writhed in response to Selina's oral tendings; and not long thenceforth came the patented spasms that signaled orgasm,

Miss Aheb's monstrously skinned yet comely body flexing and clenching in the midst of the sought-after release. Once sated, she nudged Selina off with a flick of hand. "That was wonderful, my love."

"You've changed her just as you yourself have changed," I blurted loudly, "in the atrocious tainting of your skin. It allows you to share some aspect of the Pyramidiles."

"It does far more than that!" she scolded. "It's their blessing to us, Mr. Phillips. Just as your earthly babies are 'christened' with holy water to receive the anointment of your so-called God; so too are Selina and I anointed, as the Pyramidiles give us grace by bestowing the cosmic beauty of their skin to our paltry human bodies." She held out her arms to give accentuation to her breasts' "anointment," the flawless orbs made revolting by the swirls of discolour. "But in their anointing us, we receive not only an aspect of their beauty but also the blessing of their immortality, along with other wondrous traits."

"That obscene pendant," I hastened. "Like the crystals of the chandelier, it generates a similarity to the Pyramidiles' atmosphere, correct? This grotesque light that is *not* light but somehow illuminating nonetheless."

"You're correct, indeed. It's not mere light, it's the *Abhorrescence,* whose nether-rays halt aging to all those in the midst of them. Even you, Mr. Phillips. For the time you've spent in this room as well as your time on the terrascape, you have not aged a single minute."

This, too, seemed to explain the cessation of time during the soul-searing journey to that wretched domain.

The witch-priestess was giving answer to my questions, yes, but a question even more paramount remained . . .

When?

"Exactly how many thoggs have been birthed thus far?" I asked.

Her grin couldn't have broadened any more wickedly. "Of that . . . I'll leave you to guess," and then, as if summoned by a bell-toll, the motorman made its entrance, clothed but maskless, the most salient feature of its face—that grotesque, scarlet-tipped tentacle—writhing.

"I presume it is telepathy that enables you to communicate even to a monster with no ears," I said.

"The thogg's proboscis is the nerve cluster which allows it to see and hear. But it is to the beast's *brain* that my thoughts are delivered," Miss Aheb said. "However, if you *must* know, these mental commands are reflected in the actual language of the Pyramidiles. Not words, but numerals."

"Gematria," I uttered. "The substitution of letters with their corresponding numbers. The little written record there is indicates that theirs is a language of *mathematics.*"

"I'm *impressed,* Mr. Phillips," she seemed to genuinely enthuse. "Your studies of my gods are quite extensive. I don't think in words to the motorman, for instance. I think in numbers. Were you a little brighter yourself, you might have deduced the meaning of the trolley before you even got here."

My expression clearly showed I did not understand.

"1, 8, 5, 2," she said. "One, denoting the first letter of the alphabet, Mr. Phillips."

"The letter A."

"And 8?"

"The letter H."

Her smile beamed, as the rest of the truth dropped to my gut.

"5 is E, and 2 is B," I quailed. "1,8,5,2 equals AHEB." How could I not have seen that before?

"Very good," the woman mocked. "And were I to think the numbers, 11, 9, 12, and 12, and then make an indicative gesture toward your beloved sister?"

11, 9, 12, 12, I thought desperately, then calculated each number's letter-equivalent: *"K, I, L, L . . ."*

"Yes, Mr. Phillips! Kill. The thogg would then, by my mental command, *kill* Selina. Or, how about, say, 6, 21, 3, 11?"

I quickly made the translation, and gulped, *"Fuck."*

"Um-hmm. How would you like that?" she continued to mock. "How would you like to watch the motorman *fuck* your sister?"

The thought sickened me to unto death. "I *beg* you, Miss Aheb. Don't do that. I just watched a dozen of his kind do the same."

"Indeed, or perhaps I could order the motorman to fuck *you*, Mr. Phillips." She chuckled shrilly, in a manner that actually caused the chandelier's myriad crystals to clink musically together. "The sight might very well amuse me."

"Let my sister have her freedom, and I'll consent to that," I directed.

"Ah, there you go with your chivalry again." The bright eyes within the maligned face narrowed on me. "Tell me, is that what you want more than anything? Selina's release?"

"Indisputably, yes!" Was the obscene woman toying with me, or did I stand some unfractionable chance of getting my sister out of here? I stepped boldly forward. "Let's bargain. Quid pro quo."

"So you'd like one thing exchanged for some other, hmm?" she tittered inhumanly. "You regard your sister with the utmost importance, Mr. Phillips, but surely you understand that I do as well."

"Then what could be more challenging than a wager?" I argued. "It's easy to be courageous when one has the powers of telepathy and immortality, not to mention"—I jabbed a finger toward the motorman—"the services of a thing like *that* at your beck and call. Hear me, Miss Aheb. To whatever degree this evil *Abhorrescence* has imbued you with a likeness to the Pyramidiles, you're still *human,* are you not? Humans are known to be intuitive, subjective, and often even *sporting.* You can't deny the appeal of a good wager, can you? So let's do that, Miss Aheb. Accept my challenge."

A finger dawdled over a well-sucked areola as she deliberated over my "challenge." "Win or lose, I see nothing to be gained on my part. How fair is that?"

My mind clicked like an ancient abacus, desperate for a resolving quotient. "If I win the wager, then Selina goes free, yet I stay in her stead."

Selina objected, "Oh, Morgan, I could never let you!"

"Silence!" I raised my voice to her, then returned my proposition to the grotesque madam. "I will replace her as the trolley's conductor as well as the deliverer of your necessary seminal rations via the periodic ingressions."

"Is that *all?*" she complained.

Never one given to crudity, I opened my trousers without hesitation, and displayed my genitalia which, I now had on unimpeachable authority, was larger and more enduring than that of most men. "Being a woman so carnally inclined, I would think you might find some gratifying utility . . . for *this.*"

Miss Aheb's sinister eyes went wide at the vulgarian display, just as I suspected they might.

"My," she uttered. "The rumours are no exaggeration! It was reported to me quite early, Mr. Phillips, that you are quite the sexual exemplar."

Some attendant braggadocio on my part seemed in order. "My prowess in the act of fornication reduced five of your highly experienced prostitutes to *putty* earlier in the evening."

"So I've heard, while I've also heard that the *quantity* of your dispenses of seed are most excessive." She rested her chin on her fingertips. "That would prove useful around here as well."

"And whenever you're feeling a thirst for pleasures of the *lesbian* variety, this thirst can easily be quenched by any number of lascivious harlots residing here at the club."

"You make a most interesting point . . ."

"Then it's settled," came my declaration. "*I* shall replace Selina and her duties as a servitor of the Pyramidiles."

The ill-skinned woman shrilled in amusement. "Not so fast! As you've said, Mr. Phillips. One thing in exchange of another. But

I must insist that you earn the privilege of the exchange. You've neglected to propose an actual wager."

"A physical fight," I said and re-trousered my member. I looked at her in close to a glare. "You're more than just a woman, madam. You have *superhuman* powers which would seem to level the playing field. *That* is my wager. I'll bet that I defeat you."

She guffawed. "How quickly the chivalrous gentleman turns to a cad. So you want to fight a *woman?*"

"But you're a *monstrous* woman, Miss Aheb. The odds are clearly in your favor."

"So if it's a fight you want, it's a fight you'll get," she intoned. "A fight to the death. Is that *sporting* enough for you? The way I see it, this can be the only way your mettle will be proven sufficiently enough to *earn* the exchange."

Great Pegana! I thought. *She's going to allow it!* "Yes! I want it very much!"

"But it won't be a fight against *me,* Mr. Phillips. I simply *must* insist that you fight my *motorman.*"

My spirits couldn't have plummeted any lower. "The thing is an alien monstrosity! That's hardly a fair fight!"

She coyly shrugged and *har-umphed.* "Take it or leave it; and mind you, if you leave it, I'll have you consigned to the terrascape"— she purred akin to a cat—"where the service thoggs will greatly appreciate your skills in the act of fellatio"—and now she laughed outright—"as I'm told those skills are rather *expert.*"

This seemed about as fair as the Treaty of Versailles; nevertheless, I rendered the only available reply. "I accept the challenge," and then, hoping for the element of surprise, unleashed every reflexive action within my human capability, and launched myself at the very *in*human motorman.

With all the strength and viciousness that could be tapped of my 146-pound frame, I struck blow after blow to the creature's face and mid-section, exerted choke-holds and threw finger-gouges to the hideous faceless face, and when I noted the futility of all this effort, I then stooped so low as to kick the thing repeatedly and as hard as I could in the groin . . .

All to no effect.

"Fight, damn you!" I cried, now foolishly trying to lift its bodily bulk off the floor and slam it down, but, lo, the sheer *density* of its flesh gave it an unfathomable weight. More kicks and gouges, then, the impacts of which were like striking sandbags. At one point, I even took the appalling frontal tentacle between my teeth, yet even as it was fleshy and pliable, I only succeeded in cracking two of my incisors, for this proboscis was resilient as metal. During the entirety of my assault, the uniformed thing only stood there, unmoving; and I received the impression that it was amused.

"Oh, Morgan, please!" Selina sobbed aside. "Beg Miss Aheb's pardon! I told you, the thoggs are virtually *undefeatable.*"

This I was finding out the hard way, indeed. As for begging the madam's "pardon," I realised that would prove as useless as the fight I was now giving the monstrosity. "I'm dead, either way!" came my harried shout. "But at least, I won't die on my knees!"

Meanwhile, Miss Aheb chortled from her arrogant throne. Now I had taken to breaking furniture over the thing's head; I jabbed it with a shard of broken porcelain, even tried to impale it with a snapped table leg (from an absolutely splendid Thomas Sheraton library table, by the way, circa 1790). The only result of this act was the splintering of the leg's sharpened end. Lastly, I spied on a wall-mount a sword (an authentic Toledo saber, I believe), yet when I took it down and attempted to cleave the motorman's head down the middle, the razor-sharp and exquisitely folded blade only bounced off . . .

"Oh, Mr. Phillips, you really are quite comical," the horrid woman chuckled. "The reason the thogg hasn't killed you already is simply because I haven't yet directed it to."

"Then be done with it!" I spat. "I'm ready to die!"

"Very well . . ."

No words, of course, issued from Miss Aheb's lips to trigger the motorman's violence; it was instead the merest numerical *thought,* and in the time it takes lightning to fulgurate, the boneless arms of the beast were wrapped around me, python-like; and I was dragged helplessly to the floor. Any resistance I made to push off the thing's bulk went *utterly without effect.*

It mauled me; the terrifying "hand" sliding into my mouth felt like the admission of a live octopus. Even worse, though, was the action of its other hand: it began to unbuckle its trousers . . .

Gagging, I now felt the morbid, carrotlike pudenda growing to full hardness against my belly.

Miss Aheb amusedly explained, "What you must know, Mr. Phillips, it that thoggs kill what they fight . . . and *fuck* what they kill . . ."

This charming exposition was scarcely perceived. I felt the hand fully in my mouth now and even slither a length down my throat, whereupon it swelled so in size that breathing became impossible. I sensed quite clearly that the monster meant to effect my total loss of consciousness, afterwhich it would surely commence to the task of *sodomizing me to death . . .*

As the flow of oxygen decreased, the frantic activities of my brain began to darken. It was not with any conscious regard that I must have considered something akin to this: If Miss Aheb had launched the motorman's attack merely by *thinking* the proper numerical sequence, what might happen if I do the same, remembering that their language exists as a form of substituting numbers for letters?

Fading away as I was, a thought abstractly directed toward my marauder crossed my mind; the thought was this: *4, 9, 5 . . .*

The motorman suddenly bucked, seizing up with an inexplicable rigor. Then . . .

The wretched, bone-bereft hand oozed out of my mouth as the motorman rolled off me, dead.

I struggled to regain breath and collect my thoughts after being so close to death. An errant glance upward showed, first, my sister standing tensely, hands clasped as if in prayer. Her face was flushed with relief. A scan to the right, however, showed Miss Aheb sneering from her throne, none-too-pleased.

"I must credit your industriousness, Mr. Phillips, particularly under such conditions." Her eyes smoldered. "4, 9, 5 . . . D, I, E . . ."

I rose however shakily, looking down at the dead thogg. "Surely I anticipated that the thing's mind was weaker than yours. You may have read my thoughts but I'm happy to see that you could not occlude them. You've lost the wager, Miss Aheb."

"So I have," her accent trailed off to meagerness.

I rubbed my hands together. "So what now? You asked me to prove my mettle and I have indeed done that. Now's your chance to prove yours, yes?"

Here was the moment that this entire evening of horror had built up to: I had overbound all odds but, now, would this evil matron *honour* her end of the bargain?

I wasn't sure but it seemed that the anti-light—this *Abhorrescence*—had noticeably dimmed as if it somehow paralleled her spirit's pulse . . .

"You were correct in your appeal, Mr. Phillips. All humans enjoy the sport of a wager. I suppose in a sense it's not all that different from the purpose of the Pyramidiles, who live off the psychic horror very much derived from the *sport* of torture, rape, and prolonged murder on a massive scale." She sat slumped in her grandiose seat, unenlivened and quite defeated. "It's true that I'm the ultimate traitor to the human race, as—for the last seven thousand years—I live to serve the Pyramidiles; and I will one day orchestrate the slow extermination of mankind, all for the sustenance and pleasure of my gods." Her lips drew up into a thin smile. "However, I will keep my word. You've earned your exchange; your precious sister shall go free, unharmed, and you shall take her place . . ."

Was this to be believed? I sensed yes, in spite of the desolate consequences in store for myself.

I turned to my sister. "You must leave now, Selina, and forget me."

She stood frantic. "But I can't, Morgan! I can't allow you to trade your freedom for mine!"

"You can and will. I've lived my life; now go live yours." I handed her my billfold and keys. "Here is the address for my room and the keys to the door. The rent is paid for several months, and you'll find a small sum of money hidden behind my bookshelf. It should be enough to get you on your feet."

"I can't!" she sobbed.

"Go!" I yelled back.

A macabre fugue-state seemed to overwhelm the chamber, but I knew it could only genuinely be amid my mind. In what appeared to be retarded motion, Miss Aheb came down off her chair, whereupon she took Selina by the shoulders and kissed her once. Then—

She removed my sister's pendant.

With instantaneousness, the revolting, pond-scum skin that so molested Selina's physical beauty . . . *reversed!* In only seconds her face beamed in a creamy and quite normal hue.

Miss Aheb turned Selina about and gently nudged her toward the door.

"Goodbye, my beloved sister," I bid, and suddenly what occurred to me was something more than simple relief but the resplendent positivity that so enraptured my friend Mr. Erwin. "Every day is a celebration. Never forget that. *Revel* in that celebration, Selina, while I, here in my own way, shall share in your joy . . ."

She walked shakily to the ornate door, opened it, but halted, to turn her tear-streaked face to me a final time.

I smiled as I hadn't in decades. "Go."

And she was gone.

Miss Aheb traipsed slowly about the grand chamber, as if mulling penetrative thoughts. "You seem a sincere man, Mr. Phillips, in a world where men are anything but. Your thoughts remain surprisingly clear, and I'm impressed by that. But should you ever harbour hope of escape, don't bother. Perhaps you'll one day entertain the notion that your sister will report the existence of the 1852 Club to the authorities, and they'll storm through the door and wrest back your freedom. But what you must know is that no one ever finds the club save for those I *allow* to find it."

"I'm not surprised by the intricacies of your powers, madam; rest assured, I shall never challenge them. After all . . . A deal's a deal."

She turned, then, to slowly approach me.

She snapped her fingers, and in moments, I stood in the midst of the brothel's ladies of pleasure, all of whom remained naked and raving in their slatternly appeal. One by one they undressed me of all my garb, then commenced to *re*-dress me . . .

. . . in the trousers, tunic, boots, and regulation cap of a trolley-car conductor.

That bizarre fugue, impossible as it was, rose to a steady, lamenting dirge in my head, and it was then that Miss Aheb placed the pendant about *my* neck.

"Consider yourself blessed," her lithe accent hissed. "You are the *new* conductor for the trolley."

"So be it," I croaked.

It was the delightful and very spirited tart named Ammi who, with a lascivious grin, held the mirror before my face.

The silver veins shined back . . .

Into the features of my nondescript visage the brand of the Pyramidiles had now been imbued: that nauseating swirl of swamp-foam green with corpse-white.

"From here on, you exist to serve the Pyramidiles," Miss Aheb's hellish voice echoed so very softly, and then over my face she placed the parchment mask . . .

"Go now, Conductor Phillips. The trolley is ready to depart."

Three

Hence, the sum of all my destiny's parts. I conduct the trolley now, in my ghastly mask of death, during the blackest and most silent hours of eventime. A new motorman was easily procured, identical in function—and in atrociousness—to the first. When not transporting appropriately virile guests to and from the club, or making the periodic "ingressions" to that howling terrorscape upon which the execrable Pyramidiles live to suck up like wine the horrors of countless worlds, I serve these abyssal mountains of flesh and their blasphemous, aeons-old acolyte, Isimah el-Aheb. I serve the latter quite carnally and in ways too lewd to iterate; and I serve the former quite traitorously via the inter-worldly deliveries of sperm so abundantly pilfered from the club's unsuspecting suitors. Much of that consignment, to my eternal shame, is my own, and when on one bleak day in the future two billion thoggs are unleashed upon my planet, I shudder to think how *many* of them will have been sired by me . . .

And as for the question of how long the earth shall last, I cannot estimate. Another day, perhaps, or another thousand years. Whichever the case may be, my new grotesque immortality will ensure that I am here to witness it all. As for my beloved sister, I never saw her again, and I can only, however thinly, pray to Erwin's God that she is safe, unexploited, and, above all, alive.

And in times when I am in farthest proximity from my wretched mastress (and hence farthest from her prying grey matter) I dare to entertain the hope that I may eventually condition my mind to veil its thoughts soundly enough from her psychically-clutching powers and then devise some manner by which I may destroy her and close forever this horrid ingressional rive. But until that day may dawn . . .

My name is Morgan Phillips, and I am the conductor of Trolley No. 1852.

When the sudden and rather annoying series of raps sounded from the downstairs foyer, Howard frowned up from his current work-in-progress which, upon conclusion, he believed he would entitle "The Shadow Out of Time." But, oh, how he deplored interruptions! What's more, he hoped the intrusion didn't disturb his aunt who was still feebly recuperating from a broken hip.

"Howard!" came her shrill voice. "There's someone at the—"

In the name of He Who Is Not To Be Named! "My perfectly serviceable auditory functions have left me so apprised, Auntie," he raised his voice in response. "We can at least rest assured that it's *not* the landlord, since I've paid the next six months' rent."

"What a fine, gifted boy you are, Howard . . ."

I'm forty-four and she still calls me a boy . . . He shot down the stairs, hoping to circumvent more rapping, but upon opening the door, he was taken startlingly aback by the physical presence of the visitor. Poised opposite within the doorway was a significantly handsome woman with shining, shoulder-length tresses of hair the colour of sunlight, and penetrating noon-blue eyes. Even in the long, autumn-leaf overcoat, her sonsy bosom and copious curvations were so evident, the writer's power of speech stalled outright.

"Do I have the pleasure of standing before the renowned H.P. Lovecraft?" she asked in a silken wisp of a voice.

"I . . . er, uh . . ." Not one to ordinarily be struck dumb by the vision of a notably attractive woman, the writer could only gulp ludicrously in repeated attempts to make an affirmative response. The woman's cleavage *blared* at him from the V beneath her smart collar.

"Oh, I'm so sorry, sir. Perhaps I have the wrong address . . ."

"I'm Howard Lovecraft, yes," he finally erupted, "but-but-but, I'd hardly refer to myself as renowned."

"You're too humble, sir!" she exclaimed, and then a smile that could've been painted by Rubens illuminated her flawlessly angled face. "Do pardon the interruption, Mr. Lovecraft. I'm Francine Wilcox, the publisher of *Erotesque*."

Howard nearly fell into a faint; and could do little more than stammer syllabic fragments. "I—but. The directory said. Um. *Franklin* Wilcox. I could never. Imag—"

A casual laugh as she tossed her head, piloting luscious scents off her shining hair. "Oh, no, sir, that's my brother. I only share the flat with him." She hunched her shoulders, compressing the already-awesome mammarian cleft. "It's quite chilly out, Mr. Lovecraft. If I could just impose on a smidgen more of your good nature?"

Howard felt as though he'd somehow just kicked *himself* in the back of the head. "Oh, *do* forgive me, Miss Wilcox," and with a shaking hand brought her into the foyer.

She turned to him as he closed the door. "I'm sure you're quite busy with your writing, so I won't tarry . . ."

"Oh, tarry, please, tarry all you like," his words jerked. "I'm actually taking a breather from my current bit of work."

Did those radiant blue eyes steal a glimpse to his groin? *Don't be outlandish!* he thought.

"At any rate, your wonderful submission, 'Trolley No. 1852' brought such accolades from myself and my entire editorial staff that I simply *had* to visit you in person in order to notify you of its immediate acceptance."

Howard felt petrified in jubilation, to the extent that his heart skipped a few beats. An acceptance meant . . . *Another cheque!* "Why, that's—that's—that's—"

Did the subtle accentuation of her grin indicate some cryptic signal of the lascivious? "Oh, yes, sir! Your story caused quite a row!" Like a card player's sleight of hand, she at once offered a bank cheque. "So without further delay, I'd like to give you this, with my greatest thanks."

Howard's heart skipped a few *more* beats when his eyes found the words *Pay to the order of H.P. Lovecraft the sum of $500.* So not only had the second cheque arrived, it had been, of all things, *hand-delivered!*

"I—I—I," he mumbled.

"The story will appear in next month's issue, and, well . . ." She paused as if uncomfortable. "I couldn't impose by asking . . ."

Howard finally rid himself of the proverbial frogs that had found their way to his throat. "Ask, um, what?"

"We know that authors in such popular demand as yourself have so little time for alternate demonstrations of their talent, as I'm sure you're far too busy with your *important* work to ever entertain the prospect of, say, writing for us on a regular basis—"

Howard nearly fell back against the wall.

"Say, four times a year? And for no less payment, naturally."

The frogs returned in multiplicity, and after coming close to choking on them, he croaked, "I accept . . ."

She looked beyond belief, batting her long-lashed eyes. "Thank you very much, sir," and then she opened her hand over her heart. "It's been a true honour meeting you."

Howard looked at her, agog. "You're-you're not leaving already?"

"Oh, but I couldn't impose further. I know you're terribly busy—"

"I'm *not* busy!" he came very close to shouting. *Think, you lackwit! Think!* "Um, well . . . oh! Please adjourn with me to my . . . writing chamber. I have coffee!"

Francine seemed to fully blush, and she replied in a hot gush, "I was *so* hoping you'd ask, sir."

Only when Howard had climbed half the flight's steps was he stricken by a propulsive sense of dread. *My room . . . it's—it's . . .* It stood in such unkemptness and disrepair that he didn't *dare* let her see it. There were empty bean cans all about, and myriad ginger snap crumbs, not to mention mouse droppings galore.

He cleared his throat. "But I'm afraid we'll have to take our coffee in the hall—"

"*What?*"

"You see, I wasn't expecting a guest and-and-and . . ."

"Oh, Mr. Lovecraft, please! All great artists are messy. They're too busy crafting their great art to piddle valuable time with mundane chores such as housekeeping. It's said that Michelangelo never once cleaned his floor, and in fact only cleaned *himself* a few times per year. Samuel Coleridge wrote 'Rime' in what he described as his 'happy hovel.'"

Howard turned, encouraged. "You don't say? Coleridge?"

The comely face nodded behind him. "Really, sir, don't be self-conscious over your room's appearance. In all honesty, I'd be disappointed to find it tidy. However, clean or dirty, I'd be honoured to stand in the very room where the great H.P. Lovecraft has written so many ground-breaking tales."

"Well . . . since you put it *that* way."

He brought her to the landing; whereupon, his aunt's voice sailed from the next room. "Howard! Who's that you're talking to?"

For the love of Pegana! Howard let his face stiffen to sternness. "Auntie, *please!* I'm in the midst of a consultation of import with a very noteworthy editor from New York."

"How wonderful, Howard . . ."

Next, he took a deep breath, thought, *My room probably smells more foul than the cellar of the Shunned House,* and opened his door. "Rrrrr-right this way, Miss Wilcox."

"Oh, please. Call me Francine . . ."

He stepped aside and let her pass.

Instead of gagging, or rolling her eyes, her long shapely legs took her in haste to his writing-table. She smoothed her hands, as if in adoration, over the cluttered desktop, let her fingers trace across the keys of his decades-old typing-machine, then picked up his fountain pen and held it as if it were an icon. "This is so exciting," she whispered and even appeared to have a tear in her eye. "To touch the same desk upon which so many masterpieces of horror have been composed . . . and to have in my own hands . . . the *same pen.*"

Howard didn't know what to say. *I stole the pen from the library, and the desk came from a neighbour's rubbish heap.*

"You must tell me, sir—"

"*Howard,* please."

Her cheeks turned rosy. "How did you devise such an imaginative tale as 'Trolley No. 1852?'"

Here in the light from the window, Howard took greater note of her body's voluptuous secrets beneath the smart, belted overcoat. Certainly, she wore a brassiere and blouse as well, yet he could swear that the distinct out-dents of formidable areolae were evident. "Oh," he sloughed off, "it was more creative self-cannibalism than any feat of elaborate imagination. I merely took several samplings from my *Yog-Sothian* pantheon, stripped them to the bone, and added new flesh. Old wine into new bottles? The nefarious ancient hag, Keziah Mason, was metamorphosed to the lusty-physiqued but corrupt-skinned witch-priestess Isimah el-Aheb; the planet Yuggoth became the para-dimensional terrascape; my sho*ggoths* became *thoggs;* the shimmering violet flux of 'Dreams in the Witch-House' became the *Abhorrescence;* and my 'daemon-sultan' Azathoth who lives lifelessly at the pith of Chaos became the Pyramidiles." Howard's stooped shoulders shrugged. "It was quite simple, actually."

"You're too lenient in your appraisal of your talent, Howard." She took a breath, then grinned and blushed once more. "And the *sex scenes!* I won't even *ask* how you conceived of those!"

Howard fidgeted. Delighted as he was by her charming presence and flattering air, face-to-face discourse entailing matters of licentiousness with a member of the opposite sex made him *uncomfortable.* Instead, he uttered, "Oh, they just came to me and I wrote them."

Perhaps she sensed his discomfiture, for, next, she abruptly turned her back to him and gazed through the window in the space between the swags. (Regular folk had "curtains" over their windows; poor writers had "swags": any sundry fabric that had outlived its original purpose, such as old bedsheets or holey shirts, tacked over the panes. One writer, in the distant future, would have shower-curtain liners and dollar-store beach towels over his windows, a note mentioned here only in passing.) However, Francine seemed awed. "So this is the view that the master of modern horror sees every day when he writes..."

"Why, yes, and it's a view near and dear to me," Howard said, but just as the comely woman seemed awed by the sight of west Providence, Howard remained equally awed by the sight of her jutting rump as she leaned over his writing-table. His eyes inched downward, scouring first the derriere's exquisite curves, then the legs which could only be described as absolutely and inarguably *bereft of defect*. Momentarily, her heels rose out of her shoes as she stood on tiptoes, and Howard actually cringed like a fetishist, for the action caused her gorgeously toned calves to flex . . .

"The epicenter of what you're looking at is called Federal Hill," he remarked after a gulp. "Oh, pardon me! I forgot the coffee!" and then he embarked for the alcove where the pot percolated.

When he was out of Francine's view, Howard did something he *never* did . . .

He gave his crotch a squeeze.

Oh . . . my . . .

He heard her voice as he tended to the cups.

"But, Howard, why are your swags half-closed? You'd have a much better view if you opened them more."

Howard's hands shook minutely as he poured the brew, yet as he did so, a mouse popped its head out of a toppled soda-cracker box. *Wonderful,* he thought with a frown. But he *hated* spending money on traps! To her query, however, he responded, "Oh, I suppose you're right but I never bother, in fear that the swags might fall and, hence, inundate me in dust."

She laughed. "You're so silly, Howard! But you really must let me improve this view for you . . ."

What an odd choice of words, he mused and then took the twin, aromatic cups back to his writing chamber.

He stopped cold.

The view, indeed, had been improved, as he found it impossible not to take immediate notice of two paramount changes.

One, Francine hadn't opened the swags at all but instead had closed them! She'd also turned on the shadeless incandescent lamp he used at night . . .

Two, she sat up now upon the writing-table after having shed completely her handsome overcoat, to reveal that all along she'd been utterly nude beneath . . .

"Have I improved the view for you, Howard?" her whisper flowed like some warm, ambrosian fluid.

"I . . .should say so." The mere vision of the woman's flawless nudity left Howard feeling as though he were staring down from a precipice of insurmountable height.

"Oh, Howard. Please come closer to me . . ."

In gingerly steps he did so, making every effort not to allow his shaking hands to spill the coffee. Even knowing as he did—the extreme degree by which he now violated every gentleman's law—he stared unblinking at, first, the dizzyingly full breasts whose tea-rose-pink nipples stood so gorged they even seemed to minutely *beat* with the pace of her heart; the poreless skin smooth as the finest white chocolate; then—in the most shameful departure from urbanity—the glorious mound of pubic thatch shiny as new-spun gold and the tantalizing, half-seen secret of its precious folds which clearly glimmered in anticipatory excitement.

Her face looked dreamy yet burning up in wanton intent. "Make my dream come true, Howard . . ."

Howard stammered, "But—but . . .the coffee!"

"Oh, *bugger* the coffee!" Francine whined, and so excited was she that those secret folds tucked beneath the blond private hair had leaked her equally private nectar onto the very pages of his holograph of "The Shadow Out of Time."

"I need to have the *dickens* fucked out of me," she pleaded now, "by the great H. P. Lovecraft . . ."

So upon the universal edict that the true gentleman *never* fails to oblige a lady, Howard, after setting aside the two cups of Postum, lowered his trousers and engaged himself as requested. The details of this engagement need not be elaborated upon; however, *attentive* readers will very much want to be educated as to whether or not the real Howard was possessed of a masculine endowment commensurate with that of his courageous protagonist, Mr. Morgan Phillips.

The answer to this query would be, regrettably, no, for Howard's member, when fully aroused, measured only *eleven and a half inches,* not twelve.

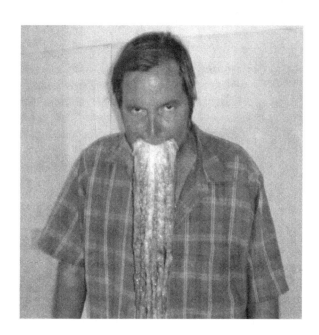

ABOUT THE AUTHOR

Edward Lee has authored close to 50 books in the field of horror; he specializes in hardcore fare. His most recent novels are LUCIFER'S LOTTERY and the Lovecraftian THE HAUNTER OF THE THRESHOLD. His movie HEADER was released on DVD by Synapse Film in June, 2009. Lee lives in Largo, Florida.

deadite press

"Brain Cheese Buffet" Edward Lee - collecting nine of Lee's most sought after tales of violence and body fluids. Featuring the Stoker nominated "Mr. Torso," the legendary gross-out piece "The Dritiphilist," the notorious "The McCrath Model SS40-C, Series S," and six more stories to test your gag reflex.

"Edward Lee's writing is fast and mean as a chain saw revved to full-tilt boogie."
   - Jack Ketchum

"Bullet Through Your Face" Edward Lee - No writer is more extreme, perverted, or gross than Edward Lee. His world is one of psychopathic redneck rapists, sex addicted demons, and semen stealing aliens. Brace yourself, the king of splatterspunk is guaranteed to shock, offend, and make you laugh until you vomit.
"Lee pulls no punches."
   - Fangoria

"The Innswich Horror" Edward Lee - In July, 1939, antiquarian and H.P. Lovecraft aficionado, Foster Morley, takes a scenic bus tour through northern Massachusetts and finds Innswich Point. There far too many similarities between this fishing village and the fictional town of Lovecraft's masterpiece, The Shadow Over Innsmouth. Join splatter king Edward Lee for a private tour of Innswich Point - a town founded on perversion, torture, and abominations from the sea.

"Slaughterhouse High" Robert Devereaux - It's prom night in the Demented States of America. A place where schools are built with secret passageways, rebellious teens get zippers installed in their mouths and genitals, and once a year one couple is slaughtered and the bits of their bodies are kept as souvenirs. But something's gone terribly wrong when the secret killer starts claiming a far higher body count than usual . . .
"A major talent!" - Poppy Z. Brite

"The Book of a Thousand Sins" Wrath James White - Welcome to a world of Zombie nymphomaniacs, psychopathic deities, voodoo surgery, and murderous priests. Where mutilation sex clubs are in vogue and torture machines are sex toys. No one makes it out alive – not even God himself.

"If Wrath James White doesn't make you cringe, you must be riding in the wrong end of a hearse."
-Jack Ketchum

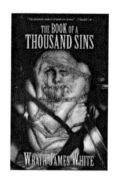

"Squid Pulp Blues" Jordan Krall - In these three bizarro-noir novellas, the reader is thrown into a world of murderers, drugs made from squid parts, deformed gun-toting veterans, and a mischievous apocalyptic donkey.

". . . with SQUID PULP BLUES, [Krall] created a wholly unique terrascape of Ibsen-like naturalism and morbidity; an extravaganza of white-trash urban/noir horror."
- Edward Lee

"Apeshit" Carlton Mellick III - Friday the 13th meets Visitor Q. Six hipster teens go to a cabin in the woods inhabited by a deformed killer. An incredibly fucked-up parody of B-horror movies with a bizarro slant

"The new gold standard in unstoppable fetus-fucking kill-freakomania . . . Genuine all-meat hardcore horror meets unadulterated Bizarro brainwarp strangeness. The results are beyond jaw-dropping, and fill me with pure, unforgivable joy." - John Skipp

"Super Fetus" Adam Pepper - Try to abort this fetus and he'll kick your ass!

"The story of a self-aware fetus whose morally bankrupt mother is desperately trying to abort him. This darkly humorous novella will surely appall and upset a sizable percentage of people who read it . . . In-your-face, allegorical social commentary."
- BarnesandNoble.com

AVAILABLE FROM AMAZON.COM

Breinigsville, PA USA
23 February 2011
256199BV00004B/182/P